Rygael's
Reward

RAYNA TYLER

ISBN: 978-1-953213-03-7

ALSO BY RAYNA TYLER

Seneca Falls Shifters

Tempting the Wild Wolf
Captivated by the Cougar
Enchanting the Bear
Enticing the Wolf
Teasing the Tiger

Ketaurran Warriors

Jardun's Embrace
Khyron's Claim
Zaedon's Kiss
Rygael's Reward
Logan's Allure
Garyck's Gift

Crescent Canyon Shifters

Engaging His Mate
Impressing His Mate
Embracing His Mate

Bradshaw Bears

Bear Appeal

CHAPTER ONE

Harper

"No" was not a word I accepted readily. In fact, I preferred not to hear it at all. Burke, the leader of the rebels who helped protect the remaining human survivors who'd been stranded on Ketaurrios, acted as if my request for help was a humorous ploy. When I narrowed my eyes to let him know I was serious, he dared to snort.

It was a good thing I was standing a few feet away and had my hands firmly planted on my hips; otherwise, I'd be tempted to punch the infuriating male in the chest. Not that I could do much damage to the broad frame covered with well-defined muscles. Being ex-military, Burke regularly trained with others to hone his fighting skills. Training that kept him in great shape.

Vince, the only other person hanging around in the gathering room of the building they referred to as headquarters, was Burke's next in command when Logan wasn't around. He was perched on the end of the long rectangular table stretched across the middle of the floor, listening to our conversation while eating one of the pytiennas I'd brought for them. He was also doing his best not to smirk between bites.

Apparently, my plan to use the sweetened flat cakes made from plants to bribe them wasn't working, which irritated me even more.

"Can't you at least go out there and talk to him?" It had been several weeks since Rygael had stubbornly refused to accept my offer of a room and insisted he return to his cave in the rocky perimeter bordering a portion of the settlement. He hadn't given me an explanation, leaving me with the impression I might have done or said something to upset him. The few times I'd asked Rygael questions about himself, he seemed uncomfortable. What little he did share wasn't much. I'd assumed it might be part of the reason he never associated with anyone in town, that his need for solitude stemmed from being different than others of his kind.

When shades of green, orange, and yellow were the standard colors for the scales covering the chest and tails of the planet's predominant race, being an albino had to be difficult. Personally, I found his silvery-white hair, and the pearlescent scales covering his chest and portions of his arms, quite attractive. His eyes, an unusual shade of pink, were even more appealing, especially when it seemed that I was the focus of his perusal.

Until recently, no one was aware of his existence. Not until he'd risked his life to rescue Melissa, one of the children in my care, from being abducted.

"Harper, I know you mean well, but I need to respect Khyron's orders." Burke scratched the dark brown stubble on his chin, and I knew he was struggling with a way to appease my request. "You know I can't force Rygael to move into town."

I wasn't happy with Khyron either. No matter how many times I urged him to persuade Rygael to relocate into town, he refused my requests. I would have thought the drezdarr, the leader of the ketaurran race, would want what was best for all his people. And as far as I was concerned, living in a rocky hole shouldn't be allowed on the list.

I couldn't stop thinking about the connection I'd felt to Rygael the moment Garyck, one of Khyron's bodyguards, also known as a vryndarr, had helped him into my spare bedroom after he'd been injured.

Ketaurrans, at least what I knew of the males, possessed an enhanced sense of smell and could scent their true mates. There'd been a few times I'd seen Rygael sniffing me when he thought I wasn't looking, and I wondered if he thought I might be his ketiorra. It wasn't as if I was looking for a male or needed one in my life. I'd done fine without one for quite some time now. At least that's what I told myself until I'd met Rygael.

Of course, any notions I'd had about the possibility of a different future disintegrated the minute he told me he was leaving and returning to his cave. No amount of arguing on my part could convince him to stay, not after Nayea, the ketaurran female who was the town's doctor had informed him that his wound was healing nicely, and he no longer had to spend his days resting.

"Who said anything about forcing? I would like you to politely insist he move into the settlement for his own safety." In this case, my interest, or so I tried to convince myself, was purely because he happened to be good with the children, the ones who'd lost their parents, and I'd taken into my home.

Realizing I wasn't his ketiorra hadn't stopped me from worrying about him living in isolation. I cared about what happened to him, even missed having him around. Ben, Gabe, Melissa, and even little Draejill, had grown attached to him. They hadn't been any happier about his departure than I had.

His visits with the children when they were playing in the woods behind our home was the only thing that made the transition a little easier for them. For me, not so much. I firmly believed that if he stayed at my place, I'd sleep better at night knowing the children were protected, and he wasn't out there all alone.

I still had nightmares every time I thought about Travis, the low-life human male who'd planned to sell Melissa into slavery. He'd made the mistake of coming to my place first, telling me he had a home for Draejill, a three-year-old half-human, half-ketaurran child, I'd also adopted. Things turned ugly when I refused to let him have the sweet little boy.

Luckily, Celeste had picked that moment to visit and ran him off. She was one of my closest friends, worked for Burke, and happened to be Khyron's mate. She was highly skilled with a blade and afterward had given me one of her daggers to keep in my boot.

To make matters worse, Travis had also pretended to be a trader to help a group of luzardee mercenaries sneak into the settlement. The luzardees were another species who lived on the planet. They were humanoidish but reminded me of two-legged lizards with flat faces and nostrils similar to a snake's. They had bald heads, black beady eyes, and though I'd never witnessed it myself, shed their skin at least once a year.

Over time, Khyron and the vryndarr had made quite a few enemies. The luzardees had come here hoping to collect on the bounties posted for the males.

Travis had driven his solarveyor to the backside of the mountain ridge and found a passageway through the perimeter. While the luzardees had gone after Khyron and his friends, Travis had tried to take Melissa. He was in the process of dragging her back to his vehicle when Rygael found them and put an end to his life.

The time Rygael spent in my home recovering was the first time in what seemed like forever that I'd felt safe. I wasn't a warrior, not like my friends; Laria, Celeste, and Sloane. I didn't have any fighting skills, and my only knife-wielding abilities were performed in a kitchen. What I lacked in skills, I made up for in determination. And in this particular situation, I was committed to getting my way.

"I don't care if he stays in the extra room at my place, or here." Not only was the large wooden building used as a command center, but it also had two levels. The upper floor consisted of sleeping quarters used by Burke and some of his team. A few were left empty for the vryndarr to use when they stayed in town. The lower level was used for gatherings, meetings, and eating. It included a kitchen and a decent-sized training area.

"As long as he's not living out there." I huffed out an exasperated sigh and pointed in the general direction of Rygael's current home. "No male should have to live alone, especially not in a cave." I'd never been inside his home but didn't think being surrounded by rock walls would be very pleasant.

Burke skimmed his hand along the side of his head. "Yeah, but it's his choice, and *we* have to respect it."

"Harper, Burke's right, we can't go against Khyron's orders." Vince held another pytienna inches from his mouth as he spoke. "If you want him to stay at your place, maybe you should go ask him yourself."

I rolled my eyes. "Gee, I can't believe I didn't think of that."

My response might have caused Vince to flinch, but it didn't have the same effect a single look from Burke did. The male was a good leader and quite proficient at non-verbal communication. The steely-eyed glare he shot at Vince, a warning not to say another word, had him cringing even more.

Footsteps on the platform-type porch outside the building alerted me to a new arrival. I turned as the door opened, and Wyatt walked inside. The male was in his late forties, and with the help of his teenage son Carter, coordinated the daily trader's market. Silver streaked the sideburns of the short, dark hair combed back from his rounded face. Normally, he wore an easy-going smile, but today concern furrowed his thick brows.

"Hey, Harper, sorry for the intrusion, but I've got a

problem and need some help." His gaze swept past Vince and me, stopping when he reached Burke.

"What's going on?" Burke didn't bother to hide his relief at having a new issue to deal with.

Wyatt tapped his thigh. "It seems some items have gone missing."

"Is it possible they were misplaced?" Burke asked.

"That was my first assumption until I received similar reports from several other vendors."

Thefts were always a possibility, but it rarely happened within the settlement because of all the males Burke had working to keep the place safe. Survival on the planet was difficult, punishments usually severe. There wasn't an enforcement system or anyone to hunt down lawbreakers, but being asked to leave and never return wasn't something most traders were willing to risk.

"Sorry, Harper, but it sounds like Wyatt's problem could be serious, and I should check it out personally. I guess we'll have to discuss your request at another time." Relief laced his tone as he hurried past me and held the door open for Wyatt.

"Uh-huh," I replied sarcastically.

Once they were gone, I turned around, hoping I'd have better luck persuading Vince.

"Oh, no." He shook his hand and waved his hand. "Don't give me that look. I won't do it either."

"Fine, if you won't help me, then I'll find a way to do it myself." I snatched the half-full container of pytiennas off the table and headed outside.

"Harper, you can leave the…" I slammed the door, cutting off the rest of Vince's plea along with his pitiful groan.

CHAPTER TWO

Rygael

I stepped off the smooth bottom step of the rocky staircase leading to the upper ledge where my cavernous home was located, then crossed the stretch of sandy dirt bordering an adjacent wooded area. After spending several years alone, every path, passageway, and cave located in the mountainous area running along the back portion of the human settlement was etched into my memory.

I was also familiar with the forest that bordered Harper's place. Until recently, I had watched over the intriguing female and the young ones she cared for from a distance, and without revealing my presence.

After being injured while preventing Melissa's abduction, Harper had welcomed me into her home for medical care and recovery. Even though my time with them was short, I had grown fond of her and the children and regretted having to return to my rocky dwelling.

I hated refusing Harper's offer to remain in her home but knew it was for the best. The white of my scales and the pink of my eyes did not go unnoticed. How could I tell her my reasons for distancing myself from others had to do with my past and the rejection I had received from my own kind?

Though Harper had never displayed any disdain for my appearance, had always treated me with kindness, it did not mean others in her community would be as accepting. Personal attacks made about my looks I could handle, but I feared my differences might affect her in a bad way, and it was something I was not willing to risk. I did not, however, let it stop me from interacting with the young ones when they played in the woods.

The snap of dried twigs and the sound of Melissa's laughter was the only warning I got before she ducked beneath the thorny branches of a nearby tree and entered the clearing where I was waiting.

"Hey, Rygael," she called as she rushed toward me. She didn't bother to slow her pace as she hurled herself at my body. I was a large ketaurran male, my muscles toned from daily activity, and easily captured the child in my arms.

Hugging, something I had never experienced until I met the ten-year-old human female with tawny hair, was a normal part of her greeting. I chuckled at her delightful squeal when I lifted her off the ground. "It is good to see you too." I set her back on her feet, then patted the top of her head.

A few seconds later, a flash of white raced past us, then skidded to a stop near a boulder at the opposite side of the clearing. "Fuzzball, come back," Melissa's command was ignored by the rare creature the child had rescued and turned into a pet. The chonderra stood no higher than the middle of her legs and had a body covered with tufts of fur and violet scales.

I watched the animal flick the forked end of its long orange tongue at the rock, no doubt trying to reach whatever tiny creatures resided near the base. "I see Fuzzball still has a problem with instructions."

Melissa sighed as she toed some loose stones. "He's a lot better than he used to be." Her brown eyes met mine, and she grinned. "At least he isn't attacking your tail anymore."

I smiled down at her. "That is indeed a great improvement."

"Where are Gabe and Ben?" I asked after realizing she was out here all alone. The two male children were a couple of years older and usually looked out for Melissa by accompanying her during our visits.

"They're not coming," she said.

"Why not?" The area was more secure than it had been before Travis tried to abduct her, but I still worried about her safety and strained to keep the anxiety out of my voice.

"Because Harper came with me today," she glanced back the way she came. A few seconds later, the female who made my tail twitch and my heart race entered the clearing and strolled toward us.

"Mornin', Rygael. It's good to see you." Her green eyes sparkled when she smiled, making the cool morning breeze seem much warmer.

"You are a welcome sight as well, Harper." This was the first time since I'd left her care that we had actually spoken. I took a step forward, unable to resist sniffing the air and inhaling her irresistible aroma.

In all my years, I had never come across a female so enticing. Much to my disappointment, her long, curly auburn locks were pulled back into a long braid. I'd spent numerous nights laying on the mat in my cave, wondering what it would be like to entwine my fingers in the silky strands.

"Since I haven't seen you in a while, I thought you might like some freshly baked pytiennas." Harper held out the sealed container she was carrying.

"And I helped make them," Melissa said with a wide-toothed grin.

I was not a male who embarrassed easily, but the slender human female could bring heat to my face as well as other parts of my body. "Harper, I appreciate your thoughtfulness," I said as I took the container.

The skin surrounding the tiny dark spots lining the bridge of her nose and cheeks, which I had learned the humans called freckles, immediately reddened. In the weeks that had passed since I returned to my cave, I had fantasized many times about sharing my sleeping mat with Harper. I wondered if her cheeks would flush the same way during the throes of passion.

Parts of my body were already reacting to her, including my tail, which I struggled to keep from swishing. Allowing my thoughts to remain on the topic was dangerous, so I quickly searched for something else to distract me. "You did not need to go to any trouble."

"It wouldn't be a problem...I mean, it's just that I worry about you living out here all alone." Her smile faded as she pointed in the direction of my home.

Was she truly displeased that I had not accepted her offer to stay in her dwelling? Upsetting her was the last thing I wished to do, but I knew an apology or sharing my regret without telling her my reasons for leaving seemed worse. "Harper, I…"

"It's okay." She brushed her hand over mine, a brief touch that ignited the warmth inside me all over again. "Besides, we need to get going." She held her hand out to Melissa. "I promised Gabe and Ben I'd watch them practice today. I also want to ask Vince if he has time to work with me after he finishes their lesson."

Why would she need help from another male? And more importantly, what kind of work would he be doing with her? "What lesson?" The words came out a little sharper than I had intended.

"Celeste was teaching the boys how to wield their knives. I heard that Khyron plans to stay in Aztrashar a little longer, so Vince is filling in until she gets back."

I was well aware of Celeste's expertise with a blade and had seen her working with the young males on several occasions. Since Harper had never mentioned it before, I was surprised to hear about the desire to defend herself.

"After everything that's happened,"—Harper started walking backward, pulling a smiling Melissa with her—"I thought it would be a good idea to be prepared. Who knows, maybe I'll even learn how to fight."

Protecting all females, no matter their species, was an instinct ingrained in all ketaurran males. Did Harper not know that I watched over her and the young ones? Did she think I would not give my life to keep them all safe? Was that why she wished to learn the skills of a warrior?

"Does that mean I get to learn how to fight too?" Melissa's plea sounded hopeful.

"Maybe in a year or so?" Harper squeezed her hand, her gaze returning to me. "Anyway, it was good seeing you again. If you need anything, you know where to find me."

"See you later, Rygael." Melissa waved. "Come on, Fuzzball." She made the smacking noise I'd taught her to call him, then groaned when the animal refused to move.

"Fuzzball, go," I said in a tone that allowed no argument, and had the small creature scurrying to obey.

"Thanks, Rygael," Melissa hollered over her shoulder as she disappeared through the trees with Harper.

I should have returned to my home, but knowing Harper intended to spend time with another male, even if it was Vince, was unsettling. Instead, I paced, trying to discern the emotions urging me to storm after her.

From the moment Garyck had helped me into Harper's home, and my gaze had locked with eyes a shade of green that rivaled the planet's sunsets, I had been enchanted with her.

It was bad enough that Harper wanted to learn how to wield a blade, but fighting involved bodily contact. The thought of another male touching what I desired was more than I could bear and had me clenching my fists. I was also forced to face a reality I had tried to deny since first catching a whiff of her intoxicating scent.

Harper was my ketiorra, my true mate. And even though I was not worthy of such a wonderful and enticing creature, I wasn't about to let another male near her.

CHAPTER THREE

Harper

"Are you sure you still want to do this?" Skepticism reflected in Vince's narrowed amber eyes. "It's okay if you want to change your mind."

I'd never asked anyone to teach me how to throw a knife before, but I wasn't going to let his trepidation stop me from learning how to defend myself. My conversation with Rygael, coupled with the fact that my friends were going to be gone a lot more, made it clear I was on my own.

I knew Rygael would risk his life to help us if he could, but his cave was too far away for me to rely on him on being around when I needed him the most. What happened if someone like Travis managed to get into my home again? I didn't like feeling helpless, not when it came to protecting the children or myself.

"Why, are you afraid I'll be better than you?" I winked at Gabe and Ben, who were taking a break and sitting in the yellowish-orange sand beneath one of the few trees with a smooth, brilliant blue trunk. The boys were a year apart in age, their dark hair the only similarities in their features. They weren't related, but their friendship was stronger than most brothers.

When I'd first asked Vince for his help, I'd expected the boys to tease me and was surprised by their show of support.

"No, I figured you'd rather have Celeste teach you since she's, you know…" He swiped his hand along the side of his head.

"My friend, an expert… What?"

"Female," Ben blurted.

Vince rarely blushed, but a hint of red crept along his cheeks. "I was going to say not a male, but female works."

I knew a person's gender didn't matter to Vince or Burke when it came to training, so why did he have a problem working with me? "What difference does that make?"

"It doesn't make any difference to me, but it will definitely bother a certain male cave dweller." Vince glanced to his left, which happened to be in the same direction as Rygael's home.

"Yeah," Gabe said. "Rygael will probably kick Vince's butt if he catches him with you."

"Yep, I agree," Ben giggled.

"Hey," Vince snapped at the boys, no doubt insulted by their lack of belief in his fighting abilities.

I crossed my arms. "No one is going to get their backside kicked because you three,"— I glared at each of them in turn—"have no idea what you're talking about." I was sure if Rygael was interested in me as a female, he wouldn't have moved out.

Not only had he left, but other than making time for the children when they played in the forest, it appeared as if he'd gone out of his way to avoid me. Up until my visit earlier, which happened to be the first time I'd spoken to him in several weeks, the only updates I'd gotten on his well-being were from the children.

"Whatever you say, Harper," Vince wiggled his brows

at the boys, eliciting more giggles and irritating me even more.

Obviously, my breath was wasted on all of them. "Maybe we should get started," I huffed.

"Fine by me." Vince retrieved a blade from the sheath on his belt. "We'll use that tree over there." He picked one with thorny branches and a wide trunk, then demonstrated a throw by hitting his target with fluid precision.

Vince made it look easy, but after watching the boys practice, I knew it was a lot harder than it looked.

After retrieving the knife, he handed it to me, hilt first. "Now, you try." He moved to stand a couple of feet behind me. "You don't need to hit the same spot. Anywhere on the trunk is fine. I want to see how you throw."

"Okay," I said as I pulled back my arm, trying to mimic what I'd seen Celeste show the boys. Unfortunately, my throwing skills lacked accuracy, and the blade bounced off the trunk, then landed in the dirt near its base.

I wrinkled my nose, then walked over to retrieve the knife. "Pretty bad, huh."

"No, not at all. Most people can't even hit the tree the first time," Vince said.

I appreciated his words of encouragement, even though I believed he was only trying to be nice.

"I think you might be flicking your wrist too much. It needs to be a fluid motion as you release." Vince waited for me to return to the spot I'd been standing. "Here, let me show you." He walked up behind me, then placed a hand on my left hip and the other on my right wrist. "When you pull back,"—he moved my arm as he spoke— "you want to…"

"What do you think you are doing?" Rygael snarled through gritted teeth as he walked into the clearing, pinning Vince with a narrow-eyed glare. His fists were clenched tightly to his sides, and his tail swished back and forth rapidly.

Though I'd never seen Rygael act this way before, I'd been around enough ketaurran males to know his low, feral growl was a protective display.

"Whoa, there big guy," Vince said before I got a chance to remind Rygael about the discussion we'd had earlier. He held up his hands and backed away from me slowly. "I was only showing her how to throw, nothing else, I swear." As soon as Rygael stop moving, Vince shot an I-told-you-so look in my direction.

I wasn't concerned about Vince. He could take care of himself. I was more concerned about Gabe and Ben. They looked up to Rygael, and I was afraid they'd be frightened by his odd behavior. Though a quick glance in their direction confirmed I had nothing to worry about.

They'd both been through a lot in their young lives. Ben was more mature than most twelve-year-olds and possessed the perceptive skills of an adult. He jutted out his chin with a confident smirk. "Told ya."

I frowned, struggling to grasp the reason for Rygael's behavior. I wasn't an expert when it came to relationships, not when it involved a male from another race. Was it possible that I'd been wrong about him, that the connection I'd felt and told myself was imagined had actually been real? Even so, it didn't explain why he'd left.

I ignored my irritation and the impulse to tell him to mind his own business. From what I'd been able to glean from the conversations we'd had during his recuperation, he'd lived in his cave a long time. I still wanted him to feel comfortable about moving into the settlement, not give him another reason to maintain his solitary existence.

"He's telling the truth." I slowly stepped between the males, giving Vince my back, and drawing Rygael's attention to me. "I was having trouble with my throw, and he was showing me how to hold the blade correctly."

"But he was...touching you." The possessive tone in Rygael's voice had my pulse racing and my body temperature rising.

I wasn't sure where his comment would lead, but it wasn't something I wanted Gabe and Ben to overhear. I glanced at Vince. "Would you mind giving us a moment?"

"Not at all." He turned towards Gabe and Ben. "Come on, guys, let's take a walk." When the boys refused to get up, he glared and motioned for them to start moving.

"Geez, things were finally getting good," Gabe groaned, making the act of getting to his feet appear strenuous.

They stomped past Vince, exaggerating each step as if they'd been ordered to do some unpleasant chore. Their stomps reminded me of the way they acted every time I asked them to do their tasks.

The situation was tense, but not stressful enough to keep me from clamping my lips and hiding my amusement. Once they were gone, and I was confident they couldn't hear me, I turned back to Rygael. "Do you want to tell me what's really going on? Why do you have a problem with Vince teaching me how to defend myself, and the children?"

"Harper, you do not need to learn how to use a blade."

Actually, I did. Now that I'd started the lesson, I could see the appeal and planned to continue learning. "Really, and why not?"

He straightened his shoulders. "Because I will protect you and the young ones."

I knew ketaurran males had a thing about taking care of females, but the last thing I wanted was Rygael telling me what to do and treating me as if I was helpless. I placed my hands on my hips, my frustration rising along with the warmth on my cheeks.

"How do you plan to do that from your cave? Because I don't remember you being around when Travis tried to take Draejill." I hadn't meant to lose my temper or snap. And I definitely hadn't intended to cause the pained expression on his face.

Lately, I'd been worried about a lot of things. The

children's safety and the dangerous missions my friends were undertaking ranked at the top of the list. Both things had caused me more than one night of restless sleep and had pushed me to the point of exhaustion.

Now that I'd finally said what was on my mind, I was eager to hear his answer.

***

Rygael

When Harper told me that Draejill's safety had been threatened by Travis, I tensed. It was the first time I had heard about the occurrence. I only knew of the worthless, now dead, male's attempt to take Melissa. An effort I had personally prevented.

"I do not understand. Burke's team guards the perimeter. I have observed their diligence on many occasions." I had even assisted Marcus's males by showing them the handful of passageways that could be accessed by intruders.

I would not admit that before the attack I also spent time hiding in the woods near her dwelling to make sure no harm came to her or the young ones. And had done so for many months.

"It happened before he tried to abduct Melissa, but even so,"—she swallowed hard—"it didn't stop him from coming into my home and trying to take Draejill."

It angered me even more to hear the attempt to steal the young one had happened in her home, and that I had not been there to help her. Knowing it had taken place before I realized she was my ketiorra did not lessen the guilt rippling through my system.

During the time I had stayed with Harper, I had never seen her overreact to any situation, no matter how difficult or upsetting. It was apparent by the frustration in her voice, and the darkened pallor beneath her eyes, that something was causing her a great deal of stress.

"Harper," I murmured, then gently took her hand. "Is my living in the cave the only thing bothering you?" My overreaction to Vince's nearness had already upset her enough, and I would do anything to remove the worry from her gaze and have her smiling at me again.

She inhaled a deep breath. "Logan and Celeste used to come by regularly to check on us, but since they left for the city with Khyron, I don't feel safe, not like I use to."

"Why did you not share your thoughts with me?" I asked as if I had earned the right to be included in her affairs, which so far, I had not.

"Because the children are my responsibility, and you'd already decided to leave."

"Harper, I…" Though I could never claim her, the realization did not stop me from slipping my hand to her hip and pulling her closer. I should have walked away, but I could not. The urge to taste her lips was overwhelming. My intent to take a small sampling disappeared the moment she pressed her palms against my chest and moaned.

Now that she was in my arms, I could not resist curling my tail around the backs of her legs and fulfilling another one of my many fantasies.

I was unsure what to say after the kiss ended, so I held her in my arms, my chin resting on her head. Moments passed before she tipped her head back, her imploring green eyes holding my gaze, searching for answers to questions I was not yet ready to give. "Rygael." She placed her hand against my cheek. "You know this doesn't change anything, right? I'm still going to continue training, to do whatever I have to so I can protect the children."

I did but refused to admit it. Harper was an intelligent and strong-willed female, fierce when it came to the young ones. I had no doubt she would make a great warrior. I struggled with the urge to protect her and keep her safe. The females of my kind were not weaklings. They were capable of doing many things but had no interest in fighting. Human females were different, they had no problem learning how to wield a blade or obtaining the skills needed to defend themselves and others.

Khyron's plan to bring the humans and ketaurrans together was admirable. I understood and admired Harper's determination to better herself, but what if her decision to train eventually led to her becoming a warrior, and she decided to join her friends on their missions to prevent another war?

I did not think she would turn the children's care over to another, not unless she believed it would prevent them from being harmed. The thought of her leaving, of never seeing her again, made my chest ache.

When I did not respond, she pulled away. Without another word or a glance in my direction, she headed toward the path Vince and the young ones had taken earlier, confirming her resolve to continue her lessons, and guaranteeing that another male would be spending time with her.

The disappointment in her eyes and the loss of her touch were equally painful. Far worse than if the scales had been ripped from my body. The physical pain I could deal with. The loss of my ketiorra, I could not.

CHAPTER FOUR

Harper

Evening was approaching, the last few rays of sunlight casting a blue tint in the usually green sky. A rumble in the distance warned of an upcoming storm, which would probably hit sometime in the middle of the night and be gone by morning.

While the children finished cleaning up after our final meal for the day, I poured a cup of freegea and slipped outside to enjoy a few moments of quiet. The drink brewed from a local plant was a little bitter and had taken some getting used to. It was the closest thing the planet had to coffee back on Earth, and after my confusing encounter with Rygael earlier, I desperately needed it.

Instead of worrying about my friends and the children, my mind filled with thoughts of Rygael, and the amazing kiss we'd shared. How being in his arms and having his tail wrapped around my legs made me feel comfortable, cared for, protected. Of course, remembering every delightful detail led to thoughts of other things. Things involving my bed, and both of us being naked. None of which were ever going to happen.

I walked out onto the platform surrounding the house and headed for the bench on the side of the building that captured the most shade, the wooden planks creaking with each step.

Because of the sandy consistency in the dirt, heavy rains left behind pools of water, which sometimes caused flooding. Most of the structures in the settlement were built at least a foot off the ground and had a platform near their entrances.

As soon as I turned the corner, I almost tripped over Rygael. He was sitting on the end of a mattress, which looked more like a thin mat. His back was braced against the exterior wall, his long legs outstretched and crossed at the ankles. He'd removed the sheath containing his blade and placed it on the bench next to a large bag normally used for carrying clothes and personal items.

"Rygael, what are you doing out here?" I steadied my cup to keep the drink from sloshing over the side and spilling on top of him.

"I wish to help you keep the young ones safe." He grinned as if his actions were obvious. "And, as you pointed out, I cannot do it from my cave."

I hadn't expected him to take me literally and groaned at the exasperating male. "I was angry and shouldn't have told you that. I certainly didn't expect you to give up your home, or start sleeping out here."

He pushed to his feet, then took the cup from my hands and set it on the bench. "I am not leaving, so it appears we have a problem. Unless…"

Having him tug on a loose curl that had escaped from my braid made breathing difficult, not to mention my ability to think clearly. "Unless what?" I managed without my voice cracking.

"Unless you are willing to let me live in your home." He leaned closer and sniffed the side of my neck, his warm breath making me shiver.

It seemed strange that only a few hours had passed

since he'd gone from being content to live in his cave to wanting to be my roommate. After the way he'd reacted to Vince, I didn't think keeping the children safe was his only motivation for changing his mind. "Wait a minute." I pressed my palms against his chest and narrowed my eyes. "You're not doing this because you don't want me to learn how to throw a knife, are you?"

"No, I would never presume to tell you what to do." He cupped my cheek. "If you wish to learn, I would gladly teach you myself."

"Is there anything else I should know before..." A door slamming followed by multiple footsteps put an end to any other questions I'd planned to ask. It also had Rygael moving a couple of feet away from me.

"Hey, Rygael," Ben said as he came around the corner, followed closely by Gabe. He noticed the mat and quirked a brow. "Are you spending the night out here?"

"Can we sleep out here with you?" Gabe asked before Rygael could answer.

Melissa showed up a few seconds later. She was leading Draejill by the hand, her pet pacing, and sniffing behind them. "Ooh, can I sleep outside too?" As soon as Fuzzball spotted Rygael, he circled her legs and went straight for his tail. Luckily, Rygael was faster and caught the animal mid-pounce. "No chewing on my tail," he reprimanded, then snuggled the creature against his chest.

Even if I wanted to, which I didn't, now that the children had arrived, I wouldn't be able to send Rygael away.

"No one is sleeping outside." I picked up the mug containing the cold and untouched drink, then handed Rygael his blade. "Rygael is moving in with us."

The joyous screams coming from Gabe, Ben, and Melissa were almost deafening. Draejill was too young to understand but jumped up and down with the others. Even Fuzzball, who'd picked up on the excitement, was making an awful howling noise.

I shot Rygael a sidelong glance. "I guess it's unanimous." I waited for the children to go ahead of us. Ben leading the way with Rygael's bag, Gabe going next and dragging the makeshift bed, leaving Melissa to bring up the end with Draejill. "And apparently, too late to change your mind."

"So, it would seem."

If he had any regrets about his decision, they were replaced with a smile the instant I took his hand and pulled him toward the door.

***

Rygael

Once the young ones had gone to bed for the night, I settled into the room Harper let me use before. Surprisingly, I had no trouble adjusting to the bed's comfort or gaining several hours of rest before being startled awake by creaking floorboards. I opened my eyes to find the room cast in shadows. Judging by the dull light filtering through the gaps around the wooden covering on the only viewing pane in the room, the day would not begin for a few more hours.

Melissa stood next to my bed with Fuzzball cradled in her arms. I had been told the humans called the long, thigh-length shirt she wore a nightgown.

"You weren't sleeping, were you?" The zapharite stone she clutched in her hand provided enough light for me to see the worry on her face. Harper told me she kept a small dish containing several of the glowing rocks in each of the children's rooms in case they had bad dreams or needed to get up in the middle of the night.

I removed my covering as I sat up and swung my legs over the bed's edge, glad I had not removed my pants. If I had been alone in my cave, I would have slept without any clothes. During my previous stay, I had learned the young ones did not always respect privacy and had frequented my room often.

According to Harper, they had all lost their families during the war. Being stranded in a strange place after their exploration spaceship crashed, and knowing they had no hope of ever returning to Earth had to have been hard enough. But to become victims of a power struggle between members of the planet's ruling family not long afterward, had to have left emotional scars on each of them.

Harper had given them a home and was doing her best to make them feel important and loved. Though I was used to being alone, I understood their need to feel safe. If coming into my room unannounced helped Melissa, then I would not reprimand her for it. "Is everything all right?"

Biting her lower lip usually meant she was nervous about saying anything, so I patiently waited for her answer. "I had a bad dream, but you can't tell Gabe and Ben because they'll think I'm a baby."

"Everyone has bad dreams." The war had been hard, sometimes devastatingly painful for all the planet's inhabitants. I had suffered through plenty of my own nightmares and understood why she did not want anyone to know about them. "What was yours about?" I patted the mattress, motioning for her to climb up next to me.

She pushed Fuzzball onto my lap as she climbed up. "You have to promise not to tell first."

"I promise." I raised a brow, encouraging her to proceed.

"Okay." She sighed dramatically once Fuzzball was settled between her arms again. "It was about that guy, you know, the one who tried to take me."

I nodded. I might have prevented Melissa's abduction, but I did not stop the male from traumatizing her. "Do you have bad dreams often?"

She shook her head. "Not so much when you lived here before, but since then…"

25

It was apparent my leaving had affected the child. I inhaled a deep breath to relieve the guilt tightening my chest, then squeezed her hand. "I will never let anything happen to you, Melissa. If you are bothered by any more dreams, all you need to do is tell me, agreed?"

"Okay." She wrinkled her nose. "Do you think Fuzzball and I could sleep in here until breakfast time?"

"That would be acceptable." I stood and waited for her to lay down with the animal curled up beside her. After covering her with a blanket, I retrieved my mat from the corner where Gabe had placed it, then stretched out on the floor.

Melissa peeked her head over the edge of the bed. "Thanks, Rygael."

"It is my pleasure, young one." The smile on her face was well worth the inconvenience of giving up the comfort of my bed.

***

The few hours of rest I got after being awakened by Melissa passed quickly without her experiencing any further dreams. Once she returned to her room on the upper level, I headed to the bathing room to clean and change.

The smell of food and the sound of laughter drew me toward the opposite end of the building. Harper's dwelling was designed to accommodate more than the four young ones currently living in her home. Her gathering area had a large open doorway leading into the kitchen and a long rectangular table sitting in the middle of the room. Between the chairs placed at each end, and the bench-style seats running along each side, there was plenty of seating.

Before I could reach the kitchen, a childlike roar erupted from underneath a corner of the table. I had forgotten about Draejill's penchant for hiding under furniture, then pouncing on anyone who walked by. The three-year-old was half-human, half-ketaurran, and seemed to have grown a little since the last time I had seen him. With pale tangerine scales covering his arms, chest, and tail, he was quite adorable.

Ketaurrans preferred their hair long and did not cut it short like some of the human males did. Harper honored that side of his lineage by allowing the young one's golden hair to grow past his shoulders. Unfortunately, the silky texture he had acquired from his human parent made it difficult for a leather tie to keep the long strands secured at his nape.

"Draejill," I said in a stern voice when the young one growled and pushed aside a chair. Fuzzball was not the only one who did not heed warnings and assumed I was a toy.

Ben and Gabe entered the room carrying plates and eating utensils for the table at the same time Draejill lunged for my tail. Instead of lending assistance, they laughed relentlessly at my efforts to remove the squirming child and lift him off the ground.

"Erg'l," Draejill giggled his version of my name. "Missed you." He wrapped his small arms around my neck, nuzzling his cheek against mine. It warmed my heart, removing all thoughts of scolding him.

"Good morning, Rygael," Harper called over her shoulder as she busily prepared our meal. "Have a seat, breakfast will be ready shortly."

I pulled out a chair and placed Draejill on my lap. Though I continually told myself it was not possible, being around Harper and the young ones drew forth the desire to have a family of my own. She might be my ketiorra, but I knew better than to hope for anything more between us.

I had resigned myself to a solitary life for a reason. My own dam and sire had been disappointed by my white scales and had shunned me at a young age. The females of my kind had been no different. More than once, I had been reminded that no mate would want a male such as me, let alone risk giving birth to an offspring that might lack colorful scales.

"Hope you're hungry." Melissa smiled as she walked into the room ahead of Harper, carrying a large platter filled with strips of meat.

"I know I am." Ben hurried ahead of Gabe to take a seat before Melissa had a chance to set the food on the table.

"You still like freegea, right?" Harper asked as she set one of the two cups filled with the steaming liquid in front of me.

"Yes, thank you."

"Here, I'll take him." She held out her hands to a squirming Draejill, then sat down next to me and placed the young one on the bench to her left.

"If you're up to it,"—Harper placed some food on Draejill's plate—"I thought we could all go to the trader's market this morning."

It had been several years since I had been to a place where tradesman and crafters sold their goods. And though I lived nearby, I had never visited the one located in the settlement. I knew from experience the place would be filled with people who would gawk and whisper at the sight of me. I wanted to spare Harper and the young ones any embarrassment they might endure from being seen with me.

"What about Draejill? Do you not need someone to look after him? Perhaps I should stay behind and…"

"That won't be a problem." Harper moved the little one's drink before he could knock it over. "Jenna, the female who lives next door, has a child around the same age, and has already offered to look after him."

Once Harper had made up her mind, it was difficult to deter her from her goals. If she had already prepared for the excursion, it was obvious the devious female was ready for any objections I might give her. Even so, I was tempted to see what else she had come up with but was

28

thwarted by Melissa. "Rygael, you have to go."

"Yeah," Gabe said as he stuffed another piece of meat into his mouth and continued to talk. "It'll be fun."

Fun was not something I had much experience with. Not when I'd been forced to work in the ore mines until the war was over, then sought refuge in the caverns. I did not want to dampen their enthusiasm, and reluctantly said, "I am sure you are right."

CHAPTER FIVE

Harper

I should have known having Rygael and the children come with me to drop off Draejill and Fuzzball at Jenna's was going to take longer then I'd anticipated. Jenna enjoyed chatting, maybe a little too much. She randomly hopped from one topic to the next, many of which usually included facts about her husband and the important position he held on Marcus's team. Guarding the perimeter was a risky job, but I didn't think what one male did was more important than any of the others.

As soon as I introduced her to Rygael, and she figured out he was staying at my place, her questions were nonstop, and quickly had him tensing. I didn't want him to change his mind about going to the market, so as soon as she paused for a breath, I insisted we needed to leave.

"Sorry about Jenna," I said as soon as we were on our way. "She's the sweetest person, but does love to gossip."

"I am not familiar with the term gossip. Does it mean to talk a lot?" Rygael asked.

"Yep," Melissa said as she took his hand and walked beside him.

If Ben and Gabe had heard Rygael's question, they would have had a lot to add about Jenna's chatty personality. Luckily they were walking about ten feet ahead of us, their heads together, deep in their own conversation.

"Then the female does it well." Rygael grinned.

"Yes, she does." I giggled, glad he found humor in what I sensed had been an uncomfortable situation for him.

The remainder of the walk, which didn't take long, was filled with Melissa pointing at buildings and telling Rygael what they were and if people lived in them. Burke had selected an area on the opposite end of the settlement for visiting traders. Far enough from the local residents, yet within walking distance of my home. Actually, most everything in town could be reached on foot.

So far, the green sky appeared free of clouds and promised a day without rain. The storm I'd expected the night before had passed without leaving a trace of moisture, which meant our footwear wouldn't be coated with muddy sand by the time we finished our outing.

The planet didn't have seasonal changes in the weather. Because of the expansive sand-covered areas and mountainous terrain, it was sunny most of the time. The days were usually hot with cooler temperatures in the evening. Storms were unpredictable and moved in without little warning. When it did rain, the showers could be horrendous and cause problems for anyone driving a solarveyor, a sun-powered transport, across open terrains.

Besides Wyatt and his son Carter doing their best to keep the vendors organized, Burke also had a couple of his males walking around, prepared to intervene if there were disputes or other issues. Some of them, like Griffin, who stood near the entrance to the market, were single and lived in a barracks-type building not far from the command center.

"Morning, Harper." He pushed away from the building he was leaning against.

He was a pleasant enough guy. His narrow jaw and hawked nose didn't detract from his features, and I could see why some of the younger females in the community were drawn to him. For me, it was his manner. The way he leered made my skin itch, and I usually tried to avoid him.

"Hey, Griffin." I was forced to stop when he purposely ignored Rygael and stepped into my path.

"You know, I'd still be more than happy to give up working for Burke and move into your place to help you look after the kids."

I gripped the strap of the bag I'd brought along to carry my purchases a little tighter. This wasn't the first time I'd heard the offer or had to deal with his unwanted advances. There was only one thing he was after, and it wasn't to help me with the children. He proved my point by rolling his dark gaze along my body, lingering when he reached my breasts.

The war had left quite a few children homeless. Instead of creating an orphanage, I'd talked Burke's group into adding on to my house and could comfortably accommodate ten children. So far, Ben, Gabe, Melissa, and Draejill were the only ones the rebels had come across who'd needed my help.

Since the place was technically my home, I decided who got to reside there, and Griffin definitely wasn't on the list. Hoping to end his persistence and keep Rygael from growling at the same time, I slipped my arm through Rygael's, noting how his tensely flexed muscles immediately relaxed.

Beyond the possessive way he'd reacted when Vince touched me, and the kiss that left me in need of air, I had no idea what Rygael expected. I also wasn't sure how to describe our relationship, which so far, was nothing more than being roommates.

"I appreciate the offer, but it won't be necessary. This is Rygael, and he's staying at my place now." I didn't have a problem with letting anyone who asked know that I was proud to have Rygael living in my home. There would always be a handful of people who'd make their own assumptions and spread rumors, but because of what we'd all had to do to survive, the standards and judgments on Ketaurrios weren't the same as they had been back on Earth.

Griffin's gaze went to our joined arms, and he frowned. "Rygael, huh. I heard about you, but I was told you prefer living in a cave."

"Though my dwelling is comfortable, it lacks the warmth that only a female can provide." Rygael placed his hand over mine and smiled.

I wasn't sure if I should be surprised or impressed by Rygael's mischievous behavior and the fact that he'd insinuated we were sleeping together. If it meant no longer having to deal with Griffin's sexual innuendos, then I wasn't about to correct him.

Rygael's tail stroking the backs of my legs sent flutters to my stomach and added to my amusement. He hadn't taken his eyes off Griffin since making his comment, so I wasn't sure if he was aware of his actions.

Griffin's thin lips nearly disappeared when he gritted his teeth. Any retort he planned to make was interrupted by Melissa. "And he takes really good care of us too." She glared at Griffin, then turned a grin toward Rygael.

"Yep, he sure does." Ben and Gabe gathered beside Melissa, their arms crossed, their glares just as defiant.

"Glad to hear it," Griffin said, though his disappointed tone suggested otherwise. "I've got work to do, so I guess I'll talk to you all later." He stepped back, then glanced around as if there was somewhere else he needed to be.

"Come on, let's go." I urged our group toward my intended destination.

Most of the vendors used portable wooden tables to display whatever they were selling or trading. Since trees in this area were sparse and their thorny branches didn't provide much shade, some of them constructed makeshift awnings to protect themselves and their wares from the sun.

We didn't have to go far for me to find the person I've been looking for. Eli's table was covered with several pairs of footwear in various sizes, boots being the most prominent. There'd been times when my friends and I would reminisce about the lack of heels and dresses. Especially Celeste, who collected a new pair of boots wherever she traveled.

Clothing was made by hand, mostly out of necessity rather than fashion. The war had changed many things, even for the planet's original inhabitants. Most outfits were designed for comfort, not enhancing physical attributes, let alone femininity.

The ketaurrans were exceptional craftsmen, great at constructing buildings from stone and working metal ores into beautiful blades, which happened to be their only form of weaponry. There were no communication devices on the planet, and advanced technology was limited. Solar-powered transports being at the top of the list.

"Hey, Eli," I gave the selection another glance as I walked up to the table.

He smiled, making the wrinkles on his medium-tan skin more prominent. He'd recently cut his hair, showing more silver intermingled with the tiny black curls. "Good morning, Harper, kids, and…" He paused when his gaze landed on Rygael, then continued to stare as if he'd never seen a ketaurran before.

Not everyone who'd survived the crash that left us stranded on Ketaurrios had embraced their new life. There were some who resented the planet's inhabitants and weren't willing to co-exist with them. They viewed them as lower life forms, even going so far as to compare them to Earth lizards.

Things got worse during the war. The struggle for power, initiated by Khyron's uncle Sarus, had started shortly after our arrival. Not only did the male and his supporters take the lives of ketaurrans, but they also targeted all humans.

Once the battle was over, the bias still lingered, which prompted Khyron's collaboration with Burke and his team. He believed pulling all the planet's races together would help heal past wounds and ensure our survival.

Though Eli had never voiced a negative opinion about the ketaurrans, his odd behavior worried me. "Um, Eli, is everything okay?"

"What?" He snapped his head in my direction. "Oh, yes." He glanced back at Rygael and smiled. "You must be Harper's new friend."

"Yes, but how did you know?" Rygael asked.

"It's a small community, and one of Burke's guys mentioned that an albino had saved little Melissa here." He winked at the child. "At first, I thought he was kidding, but now…"

"Eli," I warned.

"Oh, sorry. I wasn't trying to be rude or anything. It's just that your scales are an unusual color. They're kind of unique and reminded me of pearls."

I blew out the breath I'd been holding, relieved to hear Eli's explanation. He was the only vendor that visited the settlement who crafted decent footwear, and I would have hated to take my business to someone else.

"Pearls," Rygael furrowed his brow as if he'd been insulted, but wasn't sure how.

"They're a precious gem back on Earth." I smiled, glad to know I wasn't the only one who'd noticed the similarities. "I guess that makes you handsome and special."

"You think I am handsome." Rygael grinned, proudly puffing out his chest, and making me wonder if no one had ever mentioned how good looking he really was.

"Sure, she does." Ben smirked. "Can't you tell?"

Having forgotten that the children had a tendency to be more honest than most adults, I closed my eyes and groaned.

With a chuckle, Eli saved me from further embarrassment by asking, "So, Harper, what can I do for you today?"

"The boys need new boots." I glanced at the poor condition of their current footwear. Repairing them was not an option since Ben's were so bad he'd worn a small hole above his right big toe. Gabe's weren't much better. The boys were going through a growth spurt, and keeping them clothed had turned into a challenging task.

Eli stepped around the table and eyed the boys' boots. "I think we can manage that."

"This will probably take a while." I lifted the flap on my bag, then pulled out a small container of pytiennas and handed them to Melissa. "Why don't you and Rygael see if Maggie's here today and trade these for a container of that special powder I like to use in my cooking."

Maggie was an agriculturist back on Earth. She was great with plants and dried out one whose name I couldn't pronounce into a sweetened powder. "We'll come and find you as soon as we're done here."

"Are you certain you will be all right?" Rygael glanced around, no doubt worried that Griffin might make an appearance after he left.

"I'll be fine." I gave his arm a reassuring pat. "Now go, and enjoy yourself."

Twenty minutes later, which had to be a record, the boys each had a suitable pair of boots that allowed for growth, and with any luck, would last for several months. At least, that was my hope.

As I searched for Rygael and Melissa, a young girl I'd never seen before caught my attention. Her crystalline blue eyes flickered with intelligence and seemed way too intense for a child her age. By the condition of her clothes, I worried that she might have been abandoned. She had a cap pulled over her head, the wisps of her blonde hair sticking out around the fabric's edges. Guessing by her height, I'd say the girl was around the same age as Gabe and Ben, though it was hard to tell with all the dirt smudging her cheeks.

If I hadn't been half-listening to Ben and Gabe's conversation and paying attention to her movements, I wouldn't have seen her snatch an item off the end of a table while the vendor was busy helping a customer, then tuck it inside her bulky jacket.

I had a feeling I'd found the thief Burke and Vince had been searching for. Without alerting the boys, I redirected them so I could follow her and find out where she was going.

I lost sight of her when she slipped into a walkway between two buildings, and I was afraid I'd have to stop trailing her. I might have kept going, but I wasn't about to drag Ben and Gabe with me. They'd stopped to check out a display of blades, so I walked a little farther, hoping to catch a glimpse of where she was going without losing sight of the boys.

She hadn't gone far before a tall human male with shoulder-length dark hair and stubble covering his chin stopped her by grabbing her arm. Recognition passed between them right before he leaned forward and whispered something in her ear. The anger furrowing his brow caused a panicked look on her face. She clutched the item I'd seen her tuck inside her baggy shirt with one hand and pushed against his chest with the other.

I knew most of the regular vendors who traveled from one settlement to another, but I'd never seen this male before. It was possible he was new, or that he'd recently moved into town. Even though the girl didn't look anything like the male, and my instincts were telling me there was something wrong with the scenario, I had no reason to believe they weren't related.

Confronting the child was better left to Burke. I was about to walk away and go find him but changed my mind the second the male raised his hand as if he were going to strike her. "Hey, what do you think you're doing?" The words were out of my mouth before I realized Ben and Gabe had joined me.

The male released the girl as he straightened, his shocked gaze transforming into an intense glare. "I don't think that's any of your business."

As much as I wanted to get the girl away from him, I knew I wouldn't be able to do it on my own. Judging by the girth of the male's midsection, he wasn't in great shape. He was, however, a good six inches taller and outweighed me by at least thirty pounds.

Ben, on the other hand, didn't use caution when it came to protecting someone in our family. Size didn't matter, and I had to place a hand on his shoulder to keep him from rushing to help the girl. "Maybe not, but I'm sure the male in charge here will have something to say about your behavior." Not to mention the stolen item the girl was hiding inside her shirt. "Why don't you two go find Burke or Vince?" I spoke to Ben and Gabe without taking my eyes off the male. If I didn't have trust issues with Griffin, he would have been my first choice since he was the closest. I'd also considered sending the boys after Rygael. He could be intimidating and would protect the girl, but I needed somebody in authority to handle the situation.

"No problem. I saw Burke on our way over here." Ben sneered at the male, then nudged Gabe's arm to get him to follow.

"That's really not necessary." A hint of fear replaced the anger in the male's tone.

"Well, I think it is." I had no idea what I'd do if he decided to grab the girl and run. Luckily, Burke's arrival a few minutes later saved me from having to worry about it.

"The boys said you had a problem." Burke glanced around as if he expected something more serious, then frowned at Ben and Gabe, who'd no doubt embellished what they'd told him to get him here faster.

"I think you're going to want to talk to this male about…" Rygael calling my name had me stopping to turn.

"Is everything all right?" Rygael rushed toward us, carrying Melissa. "I saw the young ones running and thought you were in trouble." He reached for me as soon as he set Melissa on the ground.

"I'm fine," I said, though the male who'd roughly handled the girl might not be once Rygael found out what happened.

Burke smirked, his gaze flickering with curiosity. "I take it you worked out that issue we discussed."

Any other time I wouldn't have cared about Burke sharing his insights, but I didn't want Rygael to know I'd tried to solicit his help. "Remember the problem Wyatt told you he was having?"

Burke's eyes widened. "Yeah, why?"

"I believe I found the source." Even though I'd witnessed the girl's offense, I didn't want to openly accuse her of stealing in front of everyone else, not until we had all the facts. I tipped my head toward the male and the girl.

"I see." Burke scrutinized the two more closely.

Since Rygael had been living in his cave until yesterday, I didn't think he knew about the thefts. Unlike the children, I wasn't worried about him asking a lot of questions. "Ben, I want you to take Melissa and Gabe back to Jenna's place and wait for us to come and get you."

"But…"

I held up my hand. "No buts, now go."

Burke patiently listened to their mumbled objections and waited for them to disappear from sight before addressing the male. "Can I ask your name and what business you have in town?" He placed his hands on his hips, tapping the hilt of his blade with his fingertips. I'd seen him use the tactic on numerous occasions. A tactic that always got results.

The male took a moment to swallow before answering. "The name's Conrad, and I'm just passing through."

"Not a trader, then?" Burke asked.

"No, I needed to get some supplies from the market before heading back on the road."

Desert areas on the planet were vast, and the settlement wasn't centrally located to any other communities. Unless someone followed the route of most traders, traveling here was out of the way.

"Is this your child?" Burke tipped his chin toward the girl.

She'd been quietly standing in the same spot since I'd interrupted them. Now that she had Burke's attention, she nervously shifted back and forth on her feet.

"No, I mean yeah, kind of," Conrad said.

"Which is it?" Burke wasn't a male to be trifled with, and when he narrowed his dark eyes, the intensity of his gaze had Conrad inching backward.

"She's an orphan. I took her in and have been looking after her."

"It's obvious you haven't been doing a very good job." I hated seeing any child being neglected, and it took all my will power not to smack him alongside the head with my bag.

"I don't think the child's welfare is any of your concern," Conrad huffed.

"Since I'm in charge here, I'm making it my business." Burke glanced at the bulge in the girl's shirt. "We have strict rules about stealing, with even harsher punishments. I'm guessing what she's got hidden under her shirt was taken without permission. If she's under your care, then it makes you responsible."

"I don't know anything about it." Conrad waved his hands, sidestepping away from the girl as if distancing himself severed any connections he had to her.

"Okay, then." Burke's gaze softened, but only a little when he spoke to the girl. "What's your name?"

"Lily." Fear squeaked out in her voice, but I had to give her credit for not cowering.

"Is what he said about your parents being gone true?"

A lot of people had lost family members during the war. It was a harsh reality we all lived with, and as unpleasant as Burke's question was, it needed to be asked. It didn't mean I had to like it or enjoy seeing her wince before giving an affirmative nod.

"Let's see what you've got inside there." Burke motioned toward her shirt.

Lily reached underneath her top, pulled out a rolled-up pair of pants that were way too big for her, and handed them to Burke.

He shook his head. "Since Conrad isn't a relative, it looks like I'm going to have to lock you up until the drezdarr returns, and you can plead your case to him."

"You can't be serious," I gasped, unwilling to believe Burke would actually be cruel to the child.

"Burke, you can't," Rygael growled and placed a consoling hand on the small of my back.

"Unless Harper has a better idea, I don't have a choice." His raised brow was all the clue I needed to guess what he really had in mind for Lily.

"She can stay with me," I said, doing my best to hide my conspiratorial grin. "I have plenty of room." Burke might have refused to help me with Rygael, but I knew he'd do everything he could to help Lily. And from what I'd witnessed so far, anything I provided would be an improvement to the care she was getting from Conrad.

Burke scratched his chin, pretending to ponder my suggestion. "I guess that would be okay." He returned his gaze to Lily. "Live with Harper, or stay in a cell. It's up to you."

She wrinkled her nose, decidedly unhappy with her choices. Her gaze, more curious than fearful, jumped from Burke to me, then to Rygael, where it lingered the longest. Finally, she pointed at me. "I guess I'll go with her."

"Good choice," Burke said. "But, I do have one stipulation."

"Which is?" I asked, ready to argue if I thought his request was going to be unreasonable.

"Lily has to return everything she took first," Burke said.

"I don't..." The panicked look Lily shot Conrad made me wonder if he knew she'd been stealing from people all along. I was inclined to believe he might have even encouraged it. By the way Burke was studying Conrad's reaction, I'd say he'd come to the same conclusion.

Burke gave Lily a stern look. "And, so you know, if you're caught taking anything else, you'll be having that meeting with the drezdarr I mentioned."

Lily nodded. "I understand." She bowed her head and stared at the ground, her tense stance relaxing a little.

It was evident by her behavior that she was afraid of Conrad. How many other times had he raised a hand to her, times when no one was around to stop him? Even though I was a stranger and she had no reason to trust me, I walked over and wrapped an arm around her shoulder. "Everything's going to be okay, I promise."

CHAPTER SIX

Rygael

Melissa, Ben, and Gabe had not been happy when Harper told them to go to Jenna's place and wait for us. The young ones could be overly dramatic, and it was hard not to find amusement in their grumbled discontent and occasional over the shoulder glares they shot at Harper as they shuffled away. She might not be their real mother, but she cared for them deeply and displayed exceptional parenting skills. If she was bothered by their actions, she did not show it.

I did not understand why she had sent them away until Burke started questioning Conrad about Lily and the items that had gone missing around the market. Lily had been exceptionally quiet during the walk to obtain the items she had taken and had done her best to avoid getting close to Conrad. I could not be certain, but I sensed there was more going on with the situation then the young one's desire to take what did not belong to her.

By the wrinkled condition of her clothes, the dirt on her cheeks, and the unpleasant smell from her body, it was apparent the child needed better care. After noting the menacing looks Conrad had given the young female, I was glad Harper interceded on her behalf and had offered Lily a new home.

It hadn't taken long after Burke made his threat for Lily to divulge that the stolen goods were hidden in a solarveyor. I believed Lily was more afraid of seeing the drezdarr than she was of what Conrad might do to her. Though I knew her fears were unfounded, that Khyron would never hurt a child, I kept my opinion to myself.

As we walked, I thought about my time spent with Melissa and our enlightening discussion. I had learned that the settlements' residents walked wherever they needed to go, and any visiting vehicles were restricted to a large area of flat ground near the edge of town.

The only exception was the area in front of the rebel headquarters. She'd said it was used by very important people, which I interpreted to mean it was reserved for anyone who worked with Burke.

"Which vehicle is yours?" Burke asked Conrad after surveying the five vehicles parked in a haphazard row near the far end of the dirt-covered lot.

"It's that one over there." Conrad pointed as he walked, then slowed his pace even further. He'd been reluctant to show us to his vehicle and had made several unsuccessful attempts to persuade Burke into dealing with the stolen goods later.

I was not impressed with Conrad, nor did I trust him. The amount of perspiration on the tall male's forehead seemed excessive in comparison to the warmth of the day. For a male who professed that he wasn't involved, he continually surveyed the surrounding area as if searching for a way to escape. He wouldn't be able to get far, not with the rocky terrain bordering both sides of the road leading away from the settlement.

I was confident Burke possessed the ability to handle Conrad and was more concerned about Harper and Lily's safety. There was always the possibility he might reach for the knife strapped to his hip, try to take Lily, and harm one of them in the process. As an additional precaution, I positioned myself between him and the females once we reached the solarveyor.

"Open it," Burke said.

"Sure, no problem." Conrad pressed a sequence of buttons on a flat pad near the sealed door, then stepped back and waited for the access panel to slide open.

"Harper, I know you want to help Lily, but I'd appreciate it if you waited for us out here," Burke said.

When she looked as if she was about to argue, I squeezed her hand. "Please, for me." Even if she had training like her warrior friends, I would still insist she wait. It was bad enough that Lily would need to be present, but protecting one female versus two would be a lot easier should things go wrong once we were inside.

"Fine." The tone of her voice said we would be discussing my overprotective behavior later. Surprisingly, it was a conversation I looked forward to having.

As soon as we stepped into the control portion of the vehicle, I scanned the area to make sure there were not any other weapons the male could easily access.

"Rygael, why don't you stay here with Conrad while Lily shows me where she put the items she took," Burke said, easing the young one toward the rear of the vehicle.

"My pleasure." I sidestepped to block the entryway and make it more difficult for Conrad to leave. From where I stood, I caught a glimpse of Harper pacing with her arms crossed. I also got an unobstructed view of what Lily was doing.

The young one knelt on the metal floor in front of a lower storage unit, then slid the door open. After removing everything from the shelf, she popped out the back panel, exposing a hidden compartment, then scooted out of the way.

Burke reached inside and pulled out a couple of bins filled to the top with what appeared to be clothes, footwear, and several blades. "Well, would you look at that?" He glared at Conrad as he pushed to his feet.

"I had no idea those were there." Conrad swept his hand along the side of his head, his pale cheeks bursting with red. "I swear."

"Uh-huh." It seemed Burke didn't believe the male any more than I did, but could not accuse him of untruths without witnessing the act. Lily, on the other hand, had been caught with a pair of pants that did not belong to her.

"What did you find?" Harper asked, distracting me when her body brushed against mine as she squeezed between the entry's metal frame and me. "Oh, that's not good." She frowned at the bins sitting in the walkway.

"Harper, you were supposed to wait outside," I scolded.

"I was worried about Lily." Harper motioned for the young one to go to her. Lily did not hesitate to comply, even letting Harper pull her against her side.

"Conrad, would you mind giving me a hand with these?" Burke said, reaching for one of the bins.

"But they're not mine," he scoffed, refusing to move.

"So you've said, but I still need to return these to their rightful owners."

"Then let the lizard help you." Conrad sneered in my direction.

"He is not a lizard." Harper pushed Lily behind her and stepped between Conrad and me. I had never seen a female move so fast, or have one come to my defense. "Don't you ever call him that again." She poked him in the chest before I could pull her away from him.

I lifted her around the waist and carried her outside. After lowering her to the ground, I kept my hands firmly on her hips. "Harper, it does not matter."

"It does, and…"

I pushed several loose curls off her cheek. "Not if you are going to put yourself in harm's way to protect me."

Burke cleared his throat. "If you two are done, I could

use some help." He stood away from the solarveyor with his hand on Lily's shoulder, the bins sitting on the ground near his feet.

Conrad stood in the vehicle's entryway, scowling at Burke. "Unless there's something else, I'll be leaving." He slammed his hand against the interior wall closing the access door. A few seconds later, the vehicle rumbled to life.

"You know he had something to do with this, right?" Harper glared at the solarveyor as it pulled onto the rutted dirt road leading away from the settlement. "So, why are you letting him go?"

Burke rubbed his nape. "I'm sorry, Harper, but I have no proof. Even if Lily told me he made her do it, it's his word against hers. The best I can do is have my guys keep an eye on him if he returns."

As soon as Burke and I had picked up a bin, Harper asked, "Do you suppose you could return these things without mentioning that Lily was the one responsible for taking them?" She held up her hand before Burke could argue.

"I know it's a lot to ask, but it's a small community, and you know how rumors travel." She glanced at Lily, her green eyes filled with concern. "She won't have a chance at making a decent home here if everyone thinks she's a thief."

"I suppose I could do that, but I'm counting on both of you to look after her." Burke's gaze went from Harper and me to Lily. "And you need to stay out of trouble; otherwise, we'll be having that meeting I mentioned, understood."

"Yeah." Lily bobbed her head, then took Harper's offered hand and let her lead her back toward the market.

If Lily had been stealing to survive before Conrad took her in, teaching her new habits was going to be difficult. Besides helping her adjust to her new home, I feared the biggest hurdle Harper faced would be keeping the young one from running the first chance she got.

Burke waited for the females to move further away from us. "Rygael, I didn't want to say anything in front of Harper, but I don't trust Conrad, or believe a word of his story. I got the impression Lily was afraid of him, that there was something else going on."

"I assumed the same myself," I said.

"You might want to take some extra precautions, and keep a close eye on Lily."

I did not need an explanation to understand Burke's meaning. Conrad might have left the settlement, but it did not mean he would not return, or come looking for Lily, if for no other reason than to make sure she didn't tell Burke anything. What concerned me the most was whether or not the male would bring others with him.

CHAPTER SEVEN

Harper

Once Rygael helped Burke with the bins of stolen items, he went to get the children and Fuzzball from Jenna's place, and I headed back to my home with Lily. She stopped on the platform outside the front door. "You know I can take care of myself. I don't need handouts."

It was the most she'd said since leaving the market.

I knew taking her in was going to be difficult, gaining her trust even more challenging. I had a lot of questions about her past and her connection to Conrad but decided they could wait until she got settled. Right now, I was determined to make the transition as easy as possible. "I'm sure you can." I reached for the door.

"Then why are you taking me in?" Lily stuck out her chin defiantly, refusing to go inside.

I wanted her to feel as if being here was her choice; otherwise, she'd run as soon as she got a chance. "Because you needed a place to stay, and I didn't think you'd enjoy spending the next few weeks in a cell at headquarters, but if you'd rather stay with Burke, I can take you back."

"No." Her face paled, and she reached for my arm.

"Please, I don't want to be locked up." Her fingers trembled, and I wondered if she'd been held against her will before.

I pulled her into my arms, and surprisingly, she let me. "It'll be okay," I murmured against the top of her head. "I won't let anything happen to you, I promise."

Once she relaxed, I took a step back. "Are you ready to see your new home?"

She nodded, forcing her lips into a weak smile, then followed me inside. We'd made it as far as the middle of the gathering area before the door burst open, and Gabe, Ben, and Melissa rushed inside. The three young ones saw Lily and skidded to a stop. A few seconds later, Rygael entered carrying Draejill.

"What's she doing here?" Ben pointed at Lily, his questioning tone a little defensive.

Since the children didn't know what had transpired with Lily and Conrad at the market, I'd asked Rygael not to tell them anything until we had them all in the same room together.

I stood behind Lily with my hands on her shoulders, hoping the show of support would help her relax. "Guys, this is Lily, and she's going to be staying with us."

Though Gabe, Ben, and Melissa weren't related, they were close and treated each other as if they were siblings. Bringing someone new into a working dynamic had its risks, so I watched their reactions, searching for any signs of discontent on their expressions. When all I saw was curiosity, I continued, "Lily, you've already met Rygael." I pointed as I spoke. "That's Gabe, Ben, Melissa, and the little guy is Draejill."

Out of the three, Melissa appeared to be the most excited. Being the only girl hadn't been easy for her. Having someone close to her own age to talk to and do things with would be good for her.

Ben and Gabe eyed Lily suspiciously at first, then after sharing a typical boyish glance, they shrugged and acted as if having Lily around wasn't going to be a big deal.

"Did you lose your parents too? Is that why you're coming to stay with us?" Melissa asked.

Lily's shoulders went rigid beneath my touch. I also wanted to know what had happened to her parents, what her life had been like after the crash, and how she'd suffered because of the now-ended war.

They were answers I hoped she'd eventually share. I didn't think it would happen until we'd gained her trust, and she felt comfortable living with us. I also wanted to know about the stealing. Was it something she enjoyed doing? Had it been a result of trying to survive, or had Conrad forced her to take things for him?

Before I could change the subject, Fuzzball zipped between Ben and Melissa, not stopping until he'd reached Lily and pawed at her legs.

She squeaked, jumped to the side, and grabbed my arm. "What is that?"

Melissa hurried forward. "This is Fuzzball. He's a chonderra." She snatched the animal off the ground. "Don't worry, he won't hurt you. He only likes to chew on tails." She grinned at Rygael, getting a snort for her effort.

"You can pet him if you like." She shuffled a little closer to Lily.

Lily skeptically eyed Fuzzball, then reluctantly reached for his head. Before she could connect with his furry tufts, he stuck out his long, orange-forked tongue and licked her. Her giggle was the first happy sound I'd heard her make, and I couldn't help but laugh when Fuzzball squirmed out of Melissa's arms, forcing Lily to hold him.

"See, he likes you." Melissa skimmed her hand along the animal's back.

"I have an idea," I said. "Melissa, what do you think about sharing your room with Lily?" She still had the occasional nightmare from her encounter with Travis. There'd been a few times after hearing her scream, then holding her until she fell back asleep, I cursed the miserable male for the trauma he'd caused her. There was a good chance Lily suffered from some bad dreams of her own. Hopefully, having someone to bond with would make things easier for both of them.

"Really? I mean, yeah." Melissa grinned at me enthusiastically. "Come on, I'll show you where you'll be staying."

She waited for Lily to set Fuzzball on the ground, then took her hand and pulled her toward the stairs leading to the second level. Ben and Gabe didn't need an invitation before taking off after the girls.

"Why don't you guys give her a tour while you're at it?" I would have done it myself, but figured it would help the children to get comfortable with each other if I wasn't hovering.

"Sure," Ben said, pushing ahead of Gabe.

"Me too." Draejill patted Rygael's arm, letting him know he wanted down. As soon as his feet touched the floor, he raced after the children. Without having to be asked, Gabe stopped in the middle of the stairs, then headed back down to help Draejill.

The older children always looked out for the little guy, a rarity I appreciated. "Thanks, Gabe."

Up until now, I'd been so worried about Lily that I hadn't considered how having another child underfoot was going to impact Rygael. Getting him to stay here had been a challenge, and I didn't want to run him off after the first day. "I'm so sorry. I should have asked you first before inviting Lily into our home. Are you going to be okay with this?"

***

Rygael

Our home. I was Harper's guest, yet she treated me as if I had lived here for years, and my opinions regarding Lily mattered. I would admit that being around others did not come easily for me, and usually caused me some discomfort. But being away from my ketiorra was a far greater pain, one I had no wish to endure.

"I appreciate the consideration, but it is obvious the young one has suffered, and I can think of no one better to provide her with the stability she needs." I pressed my palm to her cheek. "I will do whatever I can to help her transition."

"And what about you?" She leaned in closer. "Do you need help adjusting as well?"

I swallowed a groan before it could escape my lips. Did the female not know how much her nearness and her words tempted me? How badly I ached for her, and wanted nothing more than to take her to my bed?

Living in the same place was proving more difficult than I had anticipated. Even now, my shaft hardened with the overwhelming need to claim her as my own. "Perhaps." I brushed my lips over hers, hoping for a repeat of the last time I dared to kiss her.

"Hey, Harper," Melissa's shout had us separating instantly. She appeared at the top of the stairs a few seconds later. "Do we have some different clothes for Lily to wear?"

Harper cleared her throat. "I should probably take care of that."

"I agree." Though I was reluctant to see her leave, I needed time for the heat surging through my body to cool and hopefully alleviate my uncomfortable situation.

"I think a bath wouldn't hurt either," Harper said to Melissa as she headed for the stairs. After reaching the second step, she grabbed the railing and paused. "Maybe when I'm done getting Lily settled in, you can give me one of those knife-throwing lessons you offered me."

After the way she stood up to Conrad, it was apparent she would not hesitate to put herself in dangerous situations no matter how much I tried to persuade her not to. Ensuring she had training was the only way I could guarantee she knew how to protect herself. "I look forward to the challenge."

"Challenge, seriously," she snapped before stomping up the remaining stairs and giving me a delightful view of her shapely backside.

It seemed getting my discomfort under control was going to take longer than I thought.

***

Once Harper had removed Lily's hat and scrubbed the dirt from her face, I discovered that she was an adorable child with curly blonde hair that made her blue eyes sparkle. She was wider and several inches taller than Melissa, making her too big to borrow any of her clothes. Harper asked Ben if he would mind loaning Lily a shirt and a pair of pants until she could take the child back to the market for more outfits.

It was mid-afternoon by the time Harper and I took the young ones to the clearing where Ben and Gabe practiced their knife-throwing lessons with Vince. Though the sky lacked any storm clouds, and sunset was several hours away, it was not overly warm.

Melissa and Lily made themselves comfortable on the ground near one tree. Ben and Gabe near another. Draejill sat between Gabe's spread legs, using the older child's chest as a pillow, his head lolled to one side as he napped. Fuzzball had also worn himself out and was stretched out on a patch of inch-high groundcover.

It did not take long for the young ones to treat Lily as if she had always been a part of their family. The acceptance seemed to help her relax and share in the occasional laughter. The loss of their parents was something all the young ones had in common. It was a bond that drew them together, and would hopefully make the transition a little easier for Lily.

If she had been on her own for a long time, the need to survive was ingrained in her nature. It would explain why she continually glanced around when she thought no one was watching, as if noting the best way to escape.

"If you're done doing that sniffing thing, do you suppose you might get around to teaching me how to throw?" Harper smiled at me over her shoulder.

I laughed. "The sniffing thing, as you call it, is quite enjoyable." Her scent was how I'd recognized her as my ketiorra, and I could not resist taking in the enticing aroma every chance I got.

"Ew, you guys are icky." Gabe wrinkled his nose. "We'd rather see some blade action, wouldn't we?" He nudged Ben with his elbow.

"Yep," Ben said.

I recognized the grin of a male who was quickly reaching the age where his opinion of females was changing. Ben might be bobbing his head in agreement, but he took an interest in the way Harper and I interacted.

Even so, I did not think they would appreciate being told it would not be long before they were sniffing after females themselves. I also realized it was a moment, along with many others, that I wished to be present for.

With a snort, I returned my attention to Harper. "View the blade as an extension of your arm." I ran my fingertip along her skin and smiled at her intake of breath. I was thrilled to see how much my touch affected her. "Pick the spot you want to hit, then pull back and release. I backed up a few steps to give her room so I could watch her throw.

Her follow-through was not bad, but the knife hit at an odd angle and bounced off the trunk.

"What kind of throw was that?" Ben teased.

Harper spun around, hands on her hips. "Hey, at least I hit the tree. And, my throw would have been a lot better if Rygael hadn't been distracting me."

"I believe I am innocent...this time." I ignored her

pretense of anger and winked at Ben and Gabe.

Gabe's laughing jostled Draejill awake. The little one rolled onto his knees. As soon as he was standing, he rubbed his eyes and said, "Hungry now."

Melissa's eyes widened, and she jumped to her feet. "Oooh, me too."

I was not surprised to hear Gabe and Ben chime in as well. The young males seemed to enjoy eating more than they did knife throwing.

"Sounds like practice is over." Harper smiled at me, then held out her hands to Draejill.

I retrieved the blade and returned it to the sheath on my hip.

"Aren't you coming?" Melissa asked when Lily remained seated.

"I'll be there in a minute." The forced smile Lily gave Melissa worried me.

"Okay." Melissa picked up Fuzzball, then raced after Ben and Gabe.

Harper had also noticed the change in Lily's behavior, her concerned gaze locking with mine.

"Go ahead, I will be along shortly," I said to Harper, then waited for her to head back towards the dwelling before taking a seat on the ground next to Lily.

"Is everything okay?" I stretched out my legs and braced my back against the tree's smooth trunk.

"I guess so." She'd picked up a discarded thorn from an overhead branch and was drawing spirals in the dirt.

"Is it possible you are uncertain whether or not you should stay?"

With the gasp, she jerked her head toward me. "How did you know?"

"Let us say it is something we have in common. I understand what it feels like to be unwanted, to feel as if you do not belong."

Her gaze shot to my arms, then my tail. "You mean because of your white scales."

"Yes." I did not think it was necessary to share the ache I had endured for years knowing my own dam and sire had not wanted me. She reminded me of Ben. Her perception, one beyond her years, equally matched his. Once again, I wondered about her past, of the things she had experienced and lost.

"At least you have this." She waved her hand in the direction of Harper's place. "I don't have anything or anyone." Her rasp was barely more than a whisper. "My family is…" She stifled a sob as she pulled her legs up to her chest, then rested her chin on her knees.

"That is not true," I said. "You have the other young ones, and me. And you very much have Harper. She is one of the fiercest yet caring females I know. She would not have asked you into her home if she did not want you here."

She rolled her head to the side to peer at me. "Really?"

I nodded as I swiped the tear from her cheek. "Maybe you should think about staying a little longer and giving this place a chance."

"Is that what you're doing?" she asked.

"It is." It only took one day with Harper and the young ones to make me want more, to change my mind about returning to the cave, and to hope for a future that did not involve being alone. "Perhaps we can do it together."

She lifted her head and smiled. "I'd like that."

"Good," I said as I pushed off the ground and held out my hand. "Then we'd better go inside before Ben and Gabe eat everything."

CHAPTER EIGHT

Rygael

A day had passed since my discussion with Lily. There were times I could tell she was nervous and uncomfortable with her surroundings. She seemed to be embracing her new life, but I sensed there was something else troubling her. Something that had nothing to do with fitting into her new home. Something I hoped she would eventually share with either Harper or me.

I was glad we had not received any reports from Burke about Conrad, but I continued to remain wary that the male would return and try to find Lily.

Lily's arrival had also had a positive effect on Melissa. The young one had not shown up in my room in the middle of the night upset by bad dreams. Though I did not suffer from nightmares, I had found sleeping difficult. The bed and location were not the problem. My frustration stemmed from thoughts of telling Harper she was my ketiorra and how she would take the news.

Allowing me to kiss her was one thing, agreeing to share my bed was another. What if she refused to accept me as her male for a lifetime bond, and asked me to leave?

I cared deeply for the female and could deal with any number of rejections, but that was not one of them.

No sooner had I forced my eyes shut then I heard a noise coming from outside near the rear of the building. I rolled on my back and strained to listen. Most of the creatures that lived in the nearby woods were not dangerous, but some were nocturnal. It was not uncommon for them to wander close to the dwelling searching for food.

Instead of the light patter of rummaging footsteps I had expected, something much heavier, something possessing two feet, crept along the wooden platform causing the planks to creak.

Since my room was on the lower level, I hoped to reach the intruder before they had a chance to gain access. I was glad the remaining sleeping quarters, including Harper's, were on the upper level. It would make them more difficult to reach if I was right about the unwanted visitor being a person.

Slipping out of bed as quietly as possible, I grabbed my blade from the nearby stand, then made my way along the hallway and toward the kitchen where the rear entrance was located.

The human dwellings were simple structures, built from natural resources. The doors and viewing panes were designed to hold up against bad weather but lacked sufficient locks to keep out unwanted visitors.

So far, I had only detected one set of footsteps and hoped whoever was outside was acting alone. As a precaution, I took one of the chairs sitting next to the table, set it at an angle, and used it to brace the front door, then grabbed the other chair and headed for the kitchen. If I had been living alone, I would not have bothered. I would have allowed the intruder to come inside, then handled them with my blade. I was not willing to let anyone get near Harper or the young ones, so preventing the access seemed to be a better plan.

A small dish of zapharite stones sat on the food preparation counter near the room's only viewing pane, which was currently covered with privacy panels so no one could see inside. The rocks emitted a blue-green glow but did not provide enough light for the entire room.

I wedged the chair against the back door in the same manner I had braced the front. I did not have long to wait after easing into the shadows. The chair rattled, and after several hard thumps, which I assumed was someone shoving against the door, I heard a frustrated groan and the sound of receding footsteps.

I remained where I was, listening for any more attempts. A few minutes later, I heard gentle footsteps coming from the opposite side of the room, and watched as Harper tiptoed across the floor, then reach for the pan she used to make her pytiennas. Either she had been awakened by my movements, which I doubted, or she had heard the intruder's attempt to come inside.

I could not decide if I should be angry at the female for not coming to get me first, or proud that she did not cower when faced with a dangerous situation. Adding more distractions to my thoughts was the sleeveless shirt barely covering her body. The thin fabric hugged her curves, the hem barely reaching her thighs, and exposing her long legs.

She crept closer to the back door and my hiding spot. "Harper."

Startled, she squeaked and spun around. Had I not ducked, the metal would have connected with my head. I wrapped my arms around her waist and pulled her back against my chest. I sniffed her enticing scent, which was laced with fear. "It is me," I whispered in her ear, hoping to calm her.

"Rygael. What are you..." She leaned forward to set the pan on the counter, then turned in my arms to face me. "I could have hurt you."

I decided not to correct her assumption, to tell her it

would have taken a lot more than being smacked with a pan to cause me any real damage. "I am more interested to hear what you are doing down here? And what you planned to do with that pan."

"I thought I heard something outside and came down to investigate." She frowned at the chair. "You heard something too, didn't you? That's why you were skulking around in here."

"Ketaurran males do not skulk. We move with stealth."

She chuckled. "So, you were stealthily skulking around the kitchen."

Amused by her humor, I shrugged. "Apparently so."

"Do you think it was Conrad who was trying to get inside, that he came back for Lily?" The concern I had heard earlier was back in her voice.

There were ways to get into the settlement undetected. I had already considered the possibility of Conrad being responsible, but until I knew for sure, I did not want her to worry. "I think Burke would have informed us if the male had returned."

"You're probably right." She relaxed against me a little more.

Now that I had her alone, her warm body pressed against mine, I was not ready to return to my room. "If it would ease your mind, I will go with you to check on the young ones?"

"Oh, they're fine. When I first heard the noise, I thought it might be Lily trying to leave, so I checked on her and Melissa. I also looked in on the boys, and they're all sleeping." She sighed. "It will be a while before I can go back to sleep. Since we're both awake, can I get you anything? Nayea makes a delicious ale, and I have some stashed away for when my friends stop by for late-night visits."

She slipped out of my arms, walked across the room, and reached for the door on one of the upper storage units. I moved behind her before she could retrieve the cylinder container sitting on the top shelf. I placed a hand on her hip and nuzzled her neck. "What I want a drink will not satisfy."

She turned, placed her palms on my chest, and bit her lower lip. "Then what will...satisfy you?"

The moment I dreaded, the possibility of rejection had finally arrived, and I had no choice other than to face it. "Harper," I placed my hand over hers. "You have shown me nothing but kindness, but there are things about my past that are unpleasant, reasons I chose to live in a cave. I do not wish to keep secrets from you, and if you want to know what they are, I will share them with you."

"I don't need to hear about your past to know you are a good male." Her green eyes sparkled with desire. "What happens now is all I care about, so tell me what you want."

When Harper and the young ones looked at me, they did not see the lack of color on my scales, nor did they treat me any differently than they would anyone else. Even the drezdarr and his males had treated me with respect.

Was it possible I had finally found the home I secretly longed for? Had the reasons I had lived in seclusion for so long and deemed myself unworthy of happiness been incorrect?

There would always be those intimidated by my differences, but maybe as Harper pointed out, it was time to push aside my fears and embrace the future. "I want my ketiorra. I want you."

***

Harper

His ketiorra. The assumption I'd dismissed when Rygael moved back to his cave had been correct. He didn't give me long to ponder what he'd said before his mouth was on mine, a possessive kiss that stole my breath and left me incapable of maintaining coherent thoughts.

He slipped his hand along my back, curling his fingers in the hair at my nape. I parted my lips and leaned in closer. Having his hardened shaft pressed against my abdomen created another kind of ache, one that only he could cure.

By the time he ended the kiss, we were both panting.

"When I learned you were my mate," his words came out in a rasp. "I should have told you, not left because I thought you would not want me." He grazed my cheek with his thumb as he pushed my hair behind my ear. "A mistake I plan to correct if you will let me."

I couldn't undo the rejections he'd suffered in the past, but I could show him how much I cared about him and wanted to be with him. "And how exactly do you plan to do that?"

"By taking you to my bed and claiming you." His grin sent heat rushing through my body. "Ketaurrans mate for life." He lifted me by the hips and set me on the edge of the counter with his hips wedged between my legs. "It is a bond that can never be broken, so if you are unsure…"

I stopped him by placing my finger against his mouth. "My answer is yes. It has been yes since the first day I met you."

He curled his hand around mine, longing filling his darkened pink gaze. "Then it seems I have a lot of time to make up for."

"Yes, you do." I slipped my arms across his shoulders and hooked my legs around his waist. "Your room is closer and less likely to get small visitors."

"I believe you are correct." He slid me off the counter as if I weighed nothing, then braced my backside with his arm.

With his throat this close to my mouth, I couldn't resist teasing his skin with my lips.

"Harper," he growled, stopping in the middle of the hallway, and pressing my back against the nearest wall. He nuzzled my neck, then grazed my earlobe with his teeth.

"If you do not stop, we will not make it to my room."

"If you say so." I nipped his collarbone, making him shudder.

"Obstinate female," he muttered, then hurried to his room. After using his tail to shut the door behind us, he dumped me in the middle of the bed.

With a giggle, I rolled onto my knees, then sat on my haunches. "I believe you mentioned something about claiming."

"So I did." He grinned, then took his time undoing the bindings on his shirt.

I wasn't sure if he thought I'd change my mind, or if he wanted to give me a chance to get used to his body. I dispelled both notions by placing my hands on his chest and brushing my fingertips across his smooth pearlescent scales.

I skimmed the scar from the knife wound Travis had given him. "This looks like it healed nicely. Does it still bother you?"

"Pain is not something I feel when you touch me." He reached for the hem of my nightshirt.

Once he pulled it over my head and tossed it aside, his lips sought mine. I'd been so caught up in the kiss that I hadn't realized he'd also removed his pants until he was urging me back on the bed.

Once he'd settled between my thighs, he paused, his gaze turning somber. "I could not have asked for a more beautiful mate." He left a scorching trail along my chest with his fingertips, which he quickly followed with gentle kisses. When he settled over my breast, he swirled his tongue around my nipple, teasing until the tip was a hardened nub, and I was moaning and squirming beneath him.

By the time he'd shifted his attention to my other breast, I was more than ready to have him inside me. I gripped the sides of his head, urging his gaze to meet mine. "Rygael, I want…"

He silenced me with a kiss. "Are you always going to be so demanding?"

"Probably," I said.

"Then I will do my best to see to your needs," he murmured as he slipped his hand between us, then guided his shaft into the sensitive area between my legs.

His movements started out slow, gradually increasing in speed and intensifying the pleasure. My body responded to his touch, to his rhythm. It didn't take long before I was close to a climax. One final thrust after he skimmed the outside of my thigh and wrapped the end of his tail around my ankle was all it took to push me over the edge and call out his name.

With a growl that rumbled from his chest, he continued to push, drawing out my orgasm, then finding his own release. Instead of collapsing on top of me, he rolled on his side, pulling me with him, his tail never leaving my ankle.

Once our hearts stopped racing, and our breathing returned to normal, he swiped the sweat-dampened hair off my cheek. "Rest, my ketiorra, because I plan to see to your needs at least one more time before the sun rises."

"Only one?" I closed my eyes and snuggled against his shoulder, letting the comforting embrace of his arms and his deep-based laughter lull me to sleep.

CHAPTER NINE

Rygael

Leaving my bed, especially with Harper in it, was the last thing I wanted to do, but the young ones would be rising soon, and once they found the chairs bracing the doors, they would have many questions.

"Harper." I twirled an auburn curl around my finger. "Are you still planning to take Melissa and Lily to the market today?" She had told me the day before that the couple who made clothes for young ones traveled to several of the human settlements, and only showed up at the market once a week.

"Uh-huh." She kept her eyes closed and snuggled closer to my side. I thought we might go after lunch."

"If you do not mind, I would like to take Ben and Gabe back to my cave to gather the remainder of my belongings."

Her eyes flew open, the green flickering with happiness. "Does that mean you've decided to stay permanently?"

"Yes, you have convinced me that no matter how difficult the future may be, it is not worth facing alone." I pressed a kiss to her forehead. "I will never leave your side again."

"I like the sound of that." After a few seconds, she wrinkled her nose. "What do you think we should do about last night?"

"Do? Did you not enjoy what we did?" I knew she had, but teased her anyway, so I could see the freckles on her cheeks darken.

She made an odd growling noise. "Of course, I enjoyed what we did. I was talking about the person who tried to break in." She propped her chin on her hands. "Shouldn't we tell Burke about what happened?"

"Since we did not see the intruder, I do not believe there is anything he can do." I caressed her arm. "But I will make sure to inform him." At first, I assumed Harper's place had been targeted by the trespasser, but what if I was wrong? What if there were others like Travis intent on stealing young ones? None of the children in the settlement would be safe.

Returning to the cave for my possessions was not the only reason I wanted Ben and Gabe to accompany me. They both practiced regularly and were becoming quite adept at wielding their blades. It would not be long before they showed an interest in other things such as hunting or even wanting to become warriors.

I believed they were old enough to learn a few things about tracking. Survival was not always easy, and they needed to be prepared for the future. Even though Harper provided them with stability, there were things they could only learn from a male. I had no idea how to be a parent but was determined to teach them whatever I could.

Having lived off the land to survive, I was a decent tracker, but not as impressive as the vryndarr. With any luck, the loose sand near the rear of the platform would still be damp from the brief rain shower we'd had the previous day, and provide me with a trail of footprints I could follow.

Harper and the young ones were now my responsibility. I was capable of protecting them, but would not put them in a situation where they could be harmed. I would risk my life to keep them safe. With any luck, our search might provide information about the person's identity, or even their location. Information I planned to pass on to Burke and his team.

"Thank you." The gentle kiss Harper placed on my lips made my tail twitch, but before I could explore her mouth further, noises filled the outside corridor.

"Hey, Rygael, are you up yet?" Melissa shouted, not waiting for an answer before opening the door. She burst into the room with Fuzzball pacing near her feet. "Do you know who put the chairs against the doors?"

Ben and Gabe piled in after her, closely followed by Lily, who was carrying Draejill.

"Crap," Harper said as she hurried to cover the top half of her body with a blanket.

"What's Harper doing in your bed?" Melissa asked. "Did she have a bad dream?"

Lily pursed her lips and shot Ben a knowing look. "Um, why don't we all go out and set the table for breakfast so they can get dressed."

"That's a good idea." Ben tugged on Melissa and Gabe's sleeves and urged them out the door.

"Thanks, Lily." Harper smiled. "We'll be right out."

"You can take your time." Lily giggled, snapped her fingers at Fuzzball to get him moving, then closed the door behind her.

"She is way too smart for her age."

I caught Harper and pulled her against my chest before she could roll out of bed. "Like you, she will be a handful for any male who tempts her."

***

Rygael

As I'd expected, the young ones revisited the topic of the chairs during the morning meal. Harper allowed me to explain the reason I used them to brace the doors. I did not want the children to live in fear, so I kept the explanation brief. My intent was for them to feel safe, yet use caution, and never go anywhere away from the dwelling alone.

I also did not want to undo the progress Lily was making by sharing my suspicions about Conrad. Once I informed them I would be making some modifications to the doors to ensure they could not be opened while everyone slept, the conversation turned playful with the usual banter and teasing.

The morning passed quickly, and as soon as Harper, Melissa, and Lily headed to Jenna's to drop off Draejill and Fuzzball on their way to the market, I gathered Ben and Gabe, then headed outside. When I followed the platform to the side of the building, instead of heading into the wooded area, Ben frowned and crossed his arms. "I thought we were going to your cave."

"We will, but there is something else I must do first. Something that requires your help."

"Oh, yeah, like what?" Gabe's skepticism was more than likely attributed to thoughts of additional chores, not what I had planned for them.

"I thought you might like to learn how to track." I remembered my days in the mines, how I had been forced to do the laborious work. I would never make the young males do anything that was not their choice. "I will understand if you are not interested."

"Are you kidding?" Ben shared a wide-toothed grin with Gabe. "Of course, we want to learn."

"Sure do," Gabe added.

I was honored by their enthusiasm. "Good, then we can start by following the trail of whoever was out here last night." I walked toward the edge of the platform. "At some point, our visitor had to step into the sand. Since you are out here a lot, there will be many footprints." I pointed to a smaller set I knew belonged to one of the children. "We are looking for prints made by an adult, which will lead away from our dwelling."

I stood back and let them study the ground, impressed that I did not need to tell them to remain on the platform as they searched so that they would not disturb anything.

Ben tapped Gabe's arm. "Those have to be Fuzzball's prints."

"I agree," Gabe said. "But what do you think made these smaller ones?"

When they both glanced in my direction, I knelt to get a better look at the tiny tracks they were questioning. "Are you familiar with crognats?"

"Yep, 'cause I got stung by one once." Gabe rubbed his arm as if the incident had happened recently.

I did not imagine there was anyone on the planet who had escaped being stung by the tiny, pale gold creatures who liked to live in cool, dark places. More than once, I had found one making itself at home underneath my bed mat when I lived in the cave.

"Fuzzball likes to eat them," Ben chuckled. "Do you think that's why the creature's tracks stop right here?"

"I would say it is a good assumption." I pushed to my feet. "Do you want to continue?"

I received a resounding "absolutely" from both of them before they moved farther along the walkway. Ben and Gabe spent the next fifteen minutes pacing and discussing what they saw along with speculating on the different sizes they found. At one point, they sat down and slipped off their own boots, holding them next to a print to make a size comparison.

"I think I found them." Ben's voice rose with excitement as he leaned forward, one hand braced against his knee.

He had identified a set of footprints that approached

and departed the dwelling in the same location. "I believe you have." I stepped off the platform, making sure not to disrupt the prints, then and motioned for Ben and Gabe to follow me.

"Are we going to see where they go?" Gabe asked.

"We are going to try." Learning by observation was important, so I held back and continued to let the boys take the lead.

They didn't go far before Ben stopped. "Um, Rygael, I think we have a problem. It looks like the trail stops here on the hard dirt."

I had hoped the tracks would take us into the wooded area near Harper's place or the outskirts of the settlement. If the intruder had been Conrad, it was the way I would have expected him to travel.

Unfortunately, the person had headed toward the center of town where the walkways were frequently traveled and worn. It meant we would not be able to do any further tracking, discover the person's identity, or learn their intended destination.

"If they went into town, does it mean it's someone we know?" Ben's question was the same one I now pondered. A question that tightened my chest and left me wary and more concerned than I had been before.

***

Harper

I was looking forward to my trip to the market with Melissa and Lily. Over the past couple of days, the girls had developed a bond, which seemed to be doing well for both of them. I remembered what it was like to be their age and didn't mind walking ahead of them.

Hearing their whispers and giggles reminded me of when I was young, and the times I'd shared things with my friends, secretive things. Things I didn't want my parents to know about.

My thoughts drifted to Ben and Gabe, and their outing with Rygael. Being a female, I could only provide so much stability for the boys. I appreciated the time Vince and Burke spared to teach the boys survival skills, but they were reaching an age where they needed a male in their life daily.

I was glad when Rygael volunteered to take them with him for the afternoon, even more thrilled to hear he planned to gather the rest of his belongings. The night we'd shared together went beyond any fantasy I'd had about the male. To finally have him admit I was his ketiorra, his lifetime mate, made all the things I'd been worrying about for weeks seem moot.

"You have to tell her. She can help." I hadn't meant to eavesdrop, but it was hard not to notice the seriousness in Melissa's tone when she spoke to Lily loud enough for me to overhear.

I didn't want to seem nosy and ask, so I slowed my pace, hoping they'd be willing to share whatever they were discussing. It only took walking the length of the hardened dirt walkway past another building before Melissa sidled up next to me. "Harper." She took my hand and pulled me to a stop. "If Lily tells you something, do you promise not to get mad at her?"

I glanced at Lily, her blue eyes watching me intently. I'd slowly been trying to gain the child's trust, and had a feeling that solidifying the bond depended on how I handled the situation.

We hadn't quite reached the market area, and there weren't a lot of people on the walkways yet, so our conversation wouldn't be overheard. I squatted down in front of her to seem less intimidating. "Lily, I don't ever want you to be afraid to tell me things. If you have a problem, even if you think you did something wrong, I promise I'll listen and do whatever I can to help."

She bit the outside of her lip, her worried frown fading.

"Okay." She nervously clasped her hands. "Remember all the stuff I showed you from the market?"

"I do."

"I only took the stuff because Conrad said he'd hurt the others if I didn't."

Remaining calm and in control of my anger was difficult. Keeping it out of my voice, so I didn't upset Lily, even harder. "Others? I placed a comforting hand on her arm. "Are you saying he has other children?"

Lily nodded, her eyes threatening to tear.

"Do you know how many?"

"I only know about Emma and Kaylee. They're only six years old, and I tried to look out for them the best I could."

"And I'm sure you did a good job too." The memories of seeing the way Conrad treated Lily was bad enough. Hearing the deplorable male had two more little girls and might be mistreating them as well made me nauseous.

She sobbed. "I was scared to tell you before because I didn't want anything to happen to them."

"But she told me, and I knew you could help," Melissa said.

"You both did the right thing by letting me know." I rose to my full height.

"Are we going to go home and tell Rygael?" Melissa asked.

"We will, but since Burke is closer, I think we need to let him know in case Conrad decides to come back." It would also give me a chance to tell Burke about last night's trespasser. If Conrad was involved and dared to show his face in the settlement again, which I strongly hoped he did, Burke would ensure he found out the location of the other children by whatever means he thought necessary.

It was too bad Logan was in the city with Khyron. From what my friends had told me, he was a lot better at extracting information. Methods that caused a lot of pain. I wasn't a bloodthirsty person, but after witnessing Conrad about to hit Lily, then hearing about the other little ones, I highly supported those methods being used on the male.

I hated to postpone getting Lily new clothes, but figuring out a way to get the children away from Conrad took precedence. "Come on." I held out my hands to both of them, then led them down a side street that would get us to the headquarters building a lot faster.

If Burke wasn't there, I could always count on someone being around who'd be able to tell me where to find him. We'd barely made it to the platform surrounding the building when Griffin walked outside, stopping in the center of the wooden walkway to keep us from going inside.

"Hey, Harper. Where are you going in such a hurry?" When he glanced around, I wondered if he was checking to see if Rygael would be joining us.

I wasn't in the mood for pleasantries or having to deal with any of his unwanted advances. Nor did I care if I sounded abrupt. "I need to find Burke. Have you seen him?"

"Sure have, but he's not here." He hitched his thumb at the door behind him. "He was meeting with some of the team. I can take you to him if you like."

"That would be great, thanks." Being around Griffin always made me uncomfortable, and I would never go anywhere alone with him. Since I had Lily and Melissa with me, I didn't think he'd try anything, so I pushed aside my apprehension and followed him.

"This way's shorter." He turned and headed in a different direction. If I hadn't been so focused on rescuing Emma and Kaylee, I might have taken the time to question Griffin's unusually helpful behavior, and not been so eager to believe that he knew where to find Burke.

By the time I realized he'd led us to a deserted area between two buildings, it was too late. Not only was the path he'd chosen rarely used, but the opposite end of the walkway was blocked by a solarveyor.

"Why did you bring us this way?" I asked, hoping that Griffin had made a wrong turn, and the dread thrumming through my body was mistaken about his intentions.

As soon as I stopped to go back the way we came, Griffin hurried to get around the girls and me to stop us. "Sorry, Harper, but I can't let you leave."

He had frightened Melissa and Lily, their small fingers gripping my hands tighter. "Why not? What's going on?" My pulse inched higher as I pondered all the possible reasons he'd lied about Burke and lured us to this location.

"All I need is the girl." His gaze went to Lily.

"Well, you can't have her." As soon as I pulled Lily and Melissa behind me, things about the intruder began to make sense. Only Conrad and the people working for Burke knew Lily was staying at my place. If Conrad had shown up in town, someone would have let me know.

"Wait a minute. Last night… That was you, wasn't it?"

"Yeah, it would have been simple to get in and out with her too." He scratched his head. "When did you start securing your doors?" When I didn't answer right away, his eyes widened, then his lips curled into a vicious sneer. "I'll bet it was the lizard, wasn't it?

"Rygael is not a lizard," Melissa snapped.

"It's okay, Melissa." I held out my arm to keep her behind me when it looked as if she was going to move closer to him.

"Griffin, why are you doing this?" I knew the chances of anyone walking by and seeing us were slim. I asked because I wanted to know and because I hoped to buy myself more time to figure a way out of this. I wasn't about to make things easy for him either and tried to put some distance between us by easing the girls back a few more steps.

"For the money, of course. It would take me six months working here to make the cradassons I'll get paid for doing this one job. There are people out there who are willing to pay a lot for children." His gaze shot toward

Melissa. "I'll bet they'd give me just as much for her too."

"You'd really sell my girls for money." It was an accusation more than a question.

"Absolutely." There was no hesitation, no remorse in his voice. "No one's coming to help, so you can stop wasting my time with all your questions." He unsheathed his blade and waved it in my direction.

"I know how to throw, and from this distance, I won't miss any of you." He wiggled his wrist. "Now, turn around and start walking toward the solarveyor."

"Not until you tell me where you're taking us?" I backed Melissa and Lily away from him even more.

"Don't worry, it's not far. We're going to meet those new friends I was telling you about." Now more than ever, I wished I'd gone with Melissa's suggestion to go home and tell Rygael about the children first.

I'd finally gotten him out of the cave, and we were working on building a life together. The thought of never seeing him again wrenched at my heart, a grip so painful it made breathing difficult.

Griffin swiped the knife at the girls. "If you two don't want anything to happen to Harper, then you'll do as I say and won't give me any trouble."

"Harper." Melissa clutched my arm and whimpered.

Lily seemed to be handling the situation a lot better than I would have expected. She moved to Melissa's other side and took her hand. "It'll be okay. Just stay close to me."

Acting bravely in a scary situation for one so young was commendable. Did her newly acquired calm stem from taking on a big sister role with Emma and Kaylee? I planned to find out, but not until after the little ones had been rescued.

Right now, I was more concerned about keeping Melissa and Lily safe. I didn't have a death wish, but I wasn't about to let him take them anywhere, not without a fight.

Once we started walking, I made sure to stay between him and the girls. As soon as we reached the solarveyor, he returned his knife to its sheath. The instant he took his eyes off us to access the vehicle's security panel, I shoved him as hard as I could. With a surprised grunt, he stumbled into the metal hull, his left shoulder hitting the hardest.

I spun, but didn't move fast enough and ended up with his hand wrapped firmly around my upper arm. "Run!" I yelled at Lily when it looked like she was going to help me. "Get Melissa out of here and find help."

As long as he was wrestling with me, he couldn't get to his knife. Lily only hesitated for a second before grabbing Melissa's hand, then tugging her in the direction that would take them back to the main part of town.

"Harper, stop struggling," Griffin growled through gritted teeth. He dug his fingers into my flesh hard enough to make me wince and stop fighting him.

"Just let me go. The girls are gone, so there's no point in keeping me here."

"I'm afraid I can't do that," he snarled.

"Why? You still have time to get out of here before they come back with help."

"It's too late." He started pulling me toward the solarveyor. "Burke will never let me stay here now, and I'm not going back to Shane's place empty-handed."

I dug in my heels, refusing to make going with him easy.

"I don't have time for your stubbornness." He stopped and glared at me. "I'd be lying if I said I hated to do this."

"Do what?" I tried to pull free, but his grip was too strong.

"This," he said with a maniacal grin.

I didn't have time to react before he spun me around, wrapping his arm around my throat, and squeezing. No matter how much I struggled or clawed his skin, I couldn't get enough air to stop my sight from blurring or the world around me from going black.

CHAPTER TEN

Rygael

After our unsuccessful attempt to find the person who tried to break into our dwelling, Ben, Gabe, and I went to my cave and retrieved the remainder of my belongings along with my tools. I had noticed several other things around Harper's place in need of repair, which I planned to address in my spare time.

"Are you sure that's going to keep them out?" Ben sat cross-legged on the wooden platform near the back door intently watching and handing me the tools I requested.

Gabe was inside supposedly doing the chores he had not completed before we left for my cave. I was not surprised by his lengthy absence. He had a tendency to stray from his goals, so I was certain he was doing more playing than actual work.

Draejill and Fuzzball were still at Jenna's place. Since the female only had one child, she and Harper had an arrangement where they would take turns watching the young ones to give each other a break.

There was still a chance whoever had tried to get inside our home might return, and with Harper, Lilly, and Melissa still at the market, I decided to use the opportunity to reinforce the doors in case our intruder made a return visit. With any luck, the modifications I planned to make would ensure that access was difficult, or nearly impossible.

Having Ben assist me reminded me of one of the more pleasant times from my youth. Lyak, an old ketaurran male from the community where I grew up, was one of the few people who did not have a problem with the lack of color on my scales. He was an exceptional craftsman and spent time teaching me his skills.

With time being a constant companion during my solitary existence, I utilized some of my days by designing tools from resources I acquired from the environment. Since they were too large to move, I decided to leave the storage unit and bed I had built in the cave. If the opportunity arose where I could sneak away with Harper, it would be nice to have a place to lay naked with my beautiful ketiorra.

Not insulted by his inquiring question, I grinned. "I would be happy to have you test it once I am through."

Ben straightened his shoulders. "Sure."

"Rygael," I heard Lily's frantic shout coming from inside. A few seconds later, Melissa also called my name, her voice just as distressed.

"I am here," I said, hurrying to find them, and at the same time wondering what could have happened to upset them. Ben raced behind me, nearly slamming into my back when I stopped in the middle of the gathering room.

"Rygael, they took her," Lily sobbed through gasps of air.

"Took who?" I asked, even though the lack of Harper's presence gave me my answer.

The red on Melissa's cheeks matched Lily's as if they had been running a great distance. She placed her hand on her chest, then gulped more air before rasping, "Harper."

I knelt in front of them. "Slow down and tell me what happened."

Lily spoke next. "We were on our way to see Burke."

Melissa nodded. "Yeah, and that's when Griffin stopped us."

"What would Griffin do that?" Gabe came stomping down the stairs from the upper level.

"He said a bad guy was going to pay him to take Lily," Melissa swiped at a tear-stained cheek.

"He tried to make all of us get into his solarveyor, but Harper shoved him into the side of the vehicle and told us to run and get help.

"So we came here," Lily said. "He grabbed Harper before she could get away, and I think he might have taken her with him."

I remembered Griffin from the market. The male had gone out of his way to let Harper know he wanted her to share his bed. If the male dared to harm Harper in any way, I would make sure he paid with his life. But first, I needed to find them. And for that, I needed a vehicle.

I decided to take the young ones with me since I didn't want to waste time stopping by Jenna's place first. The female could be trusted to look after the children, but now that an attempt had been made to take Lily, I needed a male who could keep them safe until I returned.

"Come with me," I instructed as I headed toward the open doorway on the other side of the room. They followed me without hesitation.

"Where are we going?" Ben jogged to keep up with my fast pace.

Other than Marcus, who was probably guarding the perimeter, Vince and Burke were the only other males I knew well enough to entrust with the children's care. "To find help."

***

I hoped to avoid the market and stopped at the building the males working for Burke referred to as their headquarters. Ben raced ahead of me, then called out, "they're here" after bursting inside the building. Relieved, I held the door open and waited for the rest of the young ones to enter the gathering room. Vince and Burke were sitting at the long table drinking what appeared to be ale.

Burke frowned and returned his mug to the table. "Hey, Rygael, is everything okay?"

"No, I need to borrow one of your vehicles." I strained to keep the anger and fear out of my voice.

"Why do you need a solarveyor?" he asked.

"Because one of *your* males has taken Harper."

"What are you talking about?" His feet had been propped on the end of the table, and he dropped them to the floor. "Who took Harper?"

"It was Griffin," I growled, no longer able to keep the vehemence out of my voice.

"Are you draecking kidding me?" Burke snarled.

Vince cleared his throat and tipped his head at Ben and Gabe's frowning faces.

"Sorry, guys," Burke swept his hand along the side of his head.

"It's okay. We know we're not supposed to curse, but Harper said sometimes a bad situation calls for it. I bet she'd say this is one of those times."

"I'm confused. Why do you think he took Harper?"

Melissa leaned closer to Lily. "He was supposed to take Lily, but…"

"But what?" Although Burke's stance had gone rigid, he maintained a calm voice. "And where was he supposed to take her?"

Lily glanced up at me. "Will the drezdarr get mad and lock me up if I tell?"

"Khyron is a fair male. I have never known him to punish anyone for telling the truth." I rubbed Lily between the shoulders. "Please tell Burke what he wants to know."

"Okay." She turned back to Burke. "He took her to Shane. He's the one in charge."

Burke narrowed his dark eyes. "In charge of what?"

"All the kids who are like me, the ones without parents." Lily rubbed her palms along the front of her pants. "He takes us to the different settlements, then makes us steal for him. He's really mean." She took a deep breath. "Griffin said he was going to get paid a lot of cradassons if he brought me to him."

I couldn't stop the growl that rumbled from my chest. Taking my ketiorra was bad enough, but stealing young ones for profit was a deplorable act, one which would gain Griffin no mercy when I found him.

"How many males does he have working for him?" Hearing there were more males was not going to stop me from going after Harper, but it would be helpful to know how many I would need to battle.

"Conrad, who you already met, and Ian," Lily said.

"How many other children does this Shane person have?" Burke asked.

"I heard him talking about other kids, but I've only seen Emma and Kaylee."

The thought of two more young females being treated the way Lily had made me want to hurt the males even more.

"I don't understand. If they only use children, then why take Harper?" Vince asked.

Burke furrowed his brows. "Maybe he took her to keep from getting into trouble when I found him."

I knew his explanation was meant to appease the young ones. The message in the concerned gaze he leveled at me was clear. If Shane took children, he probably did business with mercs who dealt in slavery. There was a good chance Griffin planned to sell Harper to make up the money he'd lost on Lily."

There was also a possibility that Griffin planned to keep Harper for himself. It might not be the entire reason, but I was sure his desire to bed her had played a part in his decision to take her.

"Rygael." Melissa's eyes started to tear again. "I want her back."

"Do not cry, little one." I lifted her off the ground and cuddled her to my chest. "I will bring her back. I promise."

She clutched me tightly around the neck. "I know you will." Her confident voice was muffled against my skin.

"This is all my fault. If I hadn't gotten caught, and Harper hadn't taken me in, then they wouldn't have come after me." Lily's sob tore at my heart.

I squatted down and balanced Melissa on my knee, then tipped up Lily's chin. "Harper did the right thing, and you are not to blame for the actions of bad males."

Lily sniffled and wiped her cheeks with the back of her hand. "You need to take me with you. I can help you find them."

I hesitated to respond, contemplating what might happen to Harper the longer it took me to find her. Lily's safety came first, but having her show me the way would save time. "I am not happy with the idea. I will expect you to do whatever I say, understand?"

"Uh-huh." A hint of a smile appeared on Lily's lips.

I looked up at Burke. "It is possible someone else might come looking for Lily. Can you look after the young ones and keep them safe? I will also need you to go to Jenna's place and get Draejill." I did not envy the conversation he would have to suffer through when he explained why he was getting the children instead of Harper.

"I want to go with you." Melissa slid off my knee so I could stand.

"Me too," Gabe said.

Their bravery was admirable, but I would not put anyone else's life at risk. "I am honored by your offer, but I need you both to stay here where it is safe." Ben was the oldest, protective of the others, and on the verge of arguing. "Ben, the males will need help looking after the others. Can I count on you to assist them?"

He pursed his lips for the rebuttal I knew was coming. Instead, he straightened his shoulders and nodded.

Burke patted my arm. "Vince can stay here to look after the children, but we should get going."

"I did not expect... It is not necessary for you to come with us." I took Lily's hand and followed him toward the door.

"Oh, yes, it is. I would rather not have to face Harper if something happens to you. She may not know how to fight, but she is scary when she gets mad."

I had never seen Harper lose her temper, but I had witnessed her determination on numerous occasions and knew better than to challenge her.

"Besides, I was getting a little bored." Burke flashed a mischievous grin. "I haven't gotten the chance to do anything fun since I helped the vryndarr rescue Vurell from the Quaddrien."

I didn't know much about the mission he mentioned, other than it had been successful, and their team had recovered a drug that had saved Khyron's life. There was a reason Burke was in charge of the rebels. He thrived in dangerous situations and was good at what he did.

"Then, I am grateful for your help."

CHAPTER ELEVEN

Harper

The irritating pressure on my chest below my collar bone was back. At first, I thought I'd imagined it, that it was part of the unpleasant dream I was having until I heard a little girl's voice.

Memories of Griffin and the chokehold he'd placed on my neck flashed through my mind, caused me to jolt, and force my eyes open. My head pounded, and it took a few seconds for my vision to clear.

I was lying in the middle of a hard, uncomfortable bed, which appeared to be the only piece of furniture in the room and took up most of the space. Lighting was dim, the outside view from the window blocked by strips of ragged wood secured to the surrounding frame. The wood reminded me more of bars meant to keep someone in rather than keep the sunlight out.

I had no idea how long I'd been here, but judging by the amount of sunlight peeking through the cracks, it had to be late in the day.

There were two female children, each propped on their knees on either side of me like miniature statues. They hadn't said a word or moved since I opened my eyes.

The one sitting on my left must have been responsible for poking me until I woke up.

I assumed they had to be Kaylee and Emma, the children Lily had talked about. They both had dark hair, brown eyes with thick lashes, and dirt on their rounded faces. Lily said they were six years old, but she hadn't mentioned that they were twins and quite adorable.

"Hey." The girl on my left poked me again. "Are you okay?"

I wasn't all right. I rubbed the sore portion of my throat, sure I'd end up with a bruise after what Griffin had done to me. I didn't want her to worry, so I kept my opinion about my condition and what I wanted to do to the male responsible, to myself.

The other one crossed her arms. "Stop it, Emma, I told you she was all right, so quit sticking her with your finger."

If the one on the left was Emma, then the other one had to be Kaylee.

Emma harrumphed. "Well, if she's okay, then why doesn't she say so?"

I tried not to laugh at her cute logic. "I'm fine," I said, my voice raw and crackling.

"See, Kaylee, I told you," Emma said.

Kaylee ignored her sister. "What's your name? Where did you come from? Why are you here?"

"It's Harper. I came from a settlement, and I'm a friend of Lily's." I wasn't about to tell them I'd been kidnapped.

Emma smiled, her dark eyes widening. "Lily is our friend too."

Kaylee, definitely the more skeptical of the two, squinted. "How do we know you're really Lily's friend? Can you prove it?"

"She has curly blonde hair and blue eyes," I said.

"That could be anyone." Kaylee tapped her fingers on her crossed arms.

"She is very good at taking things that don't belong to

her," I said with a wink.

"That's Lily for sure," Emma giggled.

"Okay, so if you're Lily's friend, then why isn't she with you?" Kaylee asked.

That was going to be a little tougher to answer without upsetting them. Deciding on a good answer was interrupted by the sound of loud voices coming from the other room. "What?" a deep male voice bellowed right before the door burst open. It slammed against the wall with a loud thump, making all of us jump.

"Uh-oh." Emma scampered over me to reach her sister, kneeing me in the stomach in the process.

Keeping the girls behind me, I clutched my stomach and rolled to sit on the edge of the bed. Emma and Kaylee quickly scooted forward. They pressed their bodies close together and clung to the back of my shirt.

The male who entered the room first perused me as if I were an item on display for shopping. He was tall and broad-chested. His shoulders clearing the frame, but not by much. He wasn't exactly lean, but compared to Conrad, who walked inside next, he appeared to take better care of himself.

Griffin came in last and eased to the male's left. Like a lot of males on the planet, he wore a sleeveless shirt. I was glad to see the numerous scratches covering his right wrist and arm, and know that I was responsible.

Another male with light brown hair, matching stubble covering his jaw and the upper portion of his throat, remained in the hallway, leaning against the far wall. The way he leered at me was unnerving, so I scooted a little to my right, using the first male to block his view.

"Our agreement was for the girl, not this female." He ground his teeth, spit coming out with the words.

"I'm sorry, Shane. Lily got away." Griffin glared at me as if I was to blame for my abduction.

I returned Griffin's glare with a stubborn one of my own, silently letting him know that if he'd listened to me, neither one of us would be in this predicament. Even if Griffin hadn't called Shane by his name, I would've known who he was by Lily's description of him.

"And you." Shane jerked his head toward Conrad. "If you'd done your job right to begin with, we wouldn't have this problem." The disdain-filled glance he shot in Conrad's direction made me shudder, leaving me with no doubt that he was capable of causing pain or doing despicable things to others when they didn't do what he'd asked.

"Griffin may have created a bigger problem." Conrad trying to put distance between Shane and him stopped when he reached a nearby corner.

I wanted to roll my eyes and shake my head. Listening to Conrad and Griffin was like watching two children attempting to stay out of trouble by blaming someone else. As far as I was concerned, both males deserved whatever punishment Shane decided to give them.

"Yeah, and what would that be?" Shane's scowl stretched the scars that ran along the side of his face from his cheekbone to his jaw. There were three of them, equally spaced and similar in length as if he'd been clawed by some sort of creature.

"She's the one I told you about." Conrad pointed at me. "The one who caught me with Lily and reported me o Burke."

"How unfortunate for her." It wasn't Shane's grin that made me cringe. It was his menacing tone. "So, what's the problem?"

"There was a lizard with her, one with white scales." Conrad was speaking to Shane, but he was glaring at me. "You know how they get when they think a female belongs to them."

"Are you saying that Harper is Rygael's ketiorra?" Disgust swept across Griffin's paling face, and he looked at me for confirmation.

Any other time I would proudly admit that I was his

mate, but under the circumstances, I was afraid sharing the information would make my situation worse.

"Yeah, and he won't stop looking for her until he finds her. He's not going to be happy when he sees the marks you left on her throat." Conrad smirked and hooked his thumbs on his belt. "You're pretty much a dead man if he ever finds you."

Shane tapped his chin. "You two need to get a better perspective. This could actually be a good thing for us."

"How is impending death a good thing?" Griffin asked.

"Albinos are rare, right?" Shane asked.

"Well, yeah. I've never seen one before," Conrad said.

Shane clapped his hands together. "How much money do you think the mercs would be willing to pay if we captured one alive?"

I couldn't believe what he was suggesting. The thought of Rygael being sold into slavery had a wave of nausea slamming into my stomach so hard I had to swallow several times to keep the bile from rising in my throat.

"Speaking of money," Griffin said. "I'd like to get paid for bringing you the female."

"Our deal was for the child, and you failed to uphold your end of the bargain." Shane sneered. "I believe in being fair, so I'll pay you half of what I was going to give you for Lily."

"I…"

Shane's silenced Griffin's stammer with a scowl. "If you want to walk out of here alive, you'll take my offer. And, you'll help us capture the lizard." He tapped the hilt of his blade. "Are we clear?"

I got the impression Shane didn't intend to pay Griffin or let him leave. I couldn't muster any remorse for the male or the situation his greed had created. I was more concerned about Rygael and what would happen to him if he found me.

CHAPTER TWELVE

Rygael

It had been a long time since I had operated a solarveyor, so I did not refuse Burke's offer to drive. Lily sat on the short bench running along the wall behind him. Though she pretended to be strong, I could sense her fear and wished to stay by her side should she need consoling.

Dealing with some anxiety of my own, I was unable to sit and remained standing in the control area where I could also observe the surrounding landscape. Thoughts of Harper and what she must be going through continually ran through my mind. The possibility of losing my ketiorra now that I had finally found her was unbearable. The longer it took us to reach our destination, the tighter the pressure in my chest became.

Burke took the same road Conrad used when he left the settlement a few days earlier. Once the wooded area disappeared and the plants covering the ground became sparse, Lily instructed him to take a road leading into an unfamiliar terrain comprised of sand, dirt, and various sized rock formations.

The numerous ruts covering the roadway were formed

by the weather rather than use from other vehicles. At times the road curved between flat walls of rock and occasionally bordered the edge of a deep ravine.

We had traveled for almost an hour, the silence within the confines of the control area filled with tension. Burke slowed the vehicle, drawing me from my thoughts. "Which way, Lily?"

I had been watching our progress through a side-viewing pane and looked up ahead to see the road splitting in two directions.

Lily got up from the bench and stood behind Burke with her hands clutching the back of his seat. "You need to go right."

He glanced back at her. "Are you sure?"

I understood his trepidation. Taking the wrong route would cost us valuable time. Rescuing Harper was personal for him. Not only was she his friend, but he felt responsible because one of the males under his command had betrayed him by taking her.

"Yep, there's the rock that looks like a luzardee's head." She lifted her arm and wiggled her index finger to the right.

I leaned forward to get a better glimpse of the large boulder sitting on top of the ridge running parallel to the solarveyor. The smooth rounded shape did resemble a head. After applying a little imagination to the darkened indentations on its surface, I could see the slit-like mouth and slanted eyes resembling a luzardee's. "I would have to agree with her observation."

"Turning right at the luzardee's head it is, then." Burke chuckled as he maneuvered the vehicle onto a narrow road only inches wider than the metal exterior.

We hadn't gone far before the flat, rock walls bordering our sides shifted away from us, the area on the ground wide enough for several solarveyors to sit side by side. Gaps appeared between the rock formations, forming narrow passageways.

"We're almost there." Lily gripped the seat tighter, her knuckles turning white. "Shane's house is around that curve up ahead."

"Lily, do you know if there is any other way to reach his dwelling, maybe another road?" Burke asked, slowing the vehicle even more.

"I don't think so." She wrinkled her nose. "Shane never let us out of the house except when we went to the markets, but we always went this way."

Burke came to a complete stop, then shifted in his seat to face Lily and me. "I think we should walk from here. I don't want to risk them hearing the vehicle."

"I agree," I said. "It would be better if they did not have time to prepare for our arrival." There was no way to predict how the males would react if they discovered our presence too soon. Surprise was the best way to minimize the risk of Harper and the other young ones being harmed. "We can use one of those passageways to reach the backside of the ridge and circle behind them."

"Works for me." Burke headed for an overhead storage unit at the rear of the vehicle. "Is that blade you're wearing going to be enough." When he bent over to slip a thin dagger inside his boot, I glimpsed several more sheathed blades sitting on the shelf. It seemed the male liked to be prepared.

"I have what I need." I was more adept at fighting with my body, but wouldn't hesitate to use my blade if needed. Though most of the time, it wasn't necessary.

"Then let's go." Burke returned to the control area and opened the access panel.

I placed my hand on Lily's shoulder when she started to follow him outside. "Where do you think you are going?"

"With you guys."

"It is too dangerous. I want you to stay here." I eased her away from the exit.

"But…"

"No buts," I mimicked the words and tone Harper frequently used on the other young ones.

"What am I supposed to do if someone shows up while you're gone?" She slapped her hands on her hips and stomped her foot.

I gave her arm a reassuring pat, then waited for Burke to step aside so I could hop out of the vehicle. "You will be fine as long as you stay inside." My plan was to reach the other males and take care of them long before they discovered the solarveyor.

"I still think…"

Burke cut her off by pressing the button to seal the door. "Two days, and she's already acting like Harper." He shook his head. "I can't wait to see what she's like after a month."

I headed for the gap between the rocks closest to us. "She will definitely be a challenge." One I looked for to.

**

The gap between the rock formations I had chosen led Burke and me to an area where we were able to climb to the top of the ridge that would give us a better view of Shane's dwelling without being seen.

"You do know we're being followed, right?" Burke continued to move forward as he spoke.

"I do." I had detected Lily's movements minutes ago. I should have known the stubborn female would not do what she had been told. She still blamed herself for what had happened, and I knew the only thing that would soothe her self-inflicted pain was seeing Harper alive and safe.

The climb over boulders and loose dirt had not been easy, and I was impressed that it had not deterred her. As soon as she crawled onto the ledge where Burke and I were standing, I frowned and helped her to her feet. "Were my instructions to remain in the solarveyor unclear?"

"Nooo." She bent to dust the sand off the front of her pants, then defiantly stuck out her chin. "I had to come. I'm the only family Emma and Kaylee have."

I had no doubt that she would someday make an excellent warrior, but worried about her lack of judgment when it came to dangerous situations. Until that time, I planned to do whatever I could to keep her out of harm's way. If it was even possible.

Dark clouds had formed in the distance. So far, they were not advancing in our direction, but that could always change. I released a frustrated sigh. "It appears we will have to take her with us."

"Fine," Burke said as he glared at Lily. "From here on out, you better do what you're told, or I *will* change my mind about taking you to see the drezdarr."

Lily raised a brow, seemingly undaunted by his threat. Not that I blamed her. It was evident to anyone who was paying attention that the male had developed a fondness for the young one.

I crossed to the other side of the flat surface, then knelt behind some medium-sized boulders on the ledge that overlooked a one-level structure and the area surrounding it.

"That's Shane's place," Lily said as she and Burke knelt beside me.

Most of the ground around the building was covered by sandy dirt with very few plants or trees. The rock formation we had climbed formed a perimeter near the rear of the dwelling and reached at least ten feet higher than the roof.

Luckily, accessing the area near the structure would be easy. The formation we had climbed gradually tapered off to the right and could be used to climb down to the sandy basin below.

Burke nudged Lily's shoulder with his elbow. "The solarveyor on the left is one of mine, so it looks like you were right about Griffin bringing Harper here."

"The vehicle next to it looks a lot like the one Conrad had at the traders market," I said.

"It is. I'd know it anywhere." Lily shifted so she was facing Burke and me. "So, what's the plan?"

"The plan is for you to stay here while Rygael and I go down there and find Harper," Burke said.

"But I can help."

"Lily, these males are dangerous, and they're armed. Harper would never forgive herself, or me, if something happened to you." I did not want to think about what Shane would do to Lily if he realized she was the one who showed us how to get here.

"What about Kaylee and Emma?" she asked.

"Do not worry," I said. "We will find them too, but I cannot guarantee their safety if I have to worry about you as well. Do you understand?"

"Yeah, but I don't like it."

Burke covered his mouth to conceal his amusement.

I was about to push away from the boulder when a low rumble sounded in the distance. "Do you hear that?" After glancing at the clouds and noticing no change in their location, I craned my neck to listen and was disappointed to discover that the noise belonged to another vehicle.

"Whoever is driving that solarveyor passed ours. It won't take long for Shane and the others to figure out we're out here." Burke was already scooting away from the boulders.

"Then, we should go." I moved to follow him, stopping long enough to give Lily a final warning glance.

"I know," she said, plopping her backside on the ground. "Stay here."

CHAPTER THIRTEEN

Harper

Conrad paused in the doorway after Shane and Griffin left the bedroom that had become my prison. "If you're thinking about trying to escape, don't. We're out in the middle of nowhere, and too far from the settlement to make it on foot."

I couldn't see outside, so I had no way to confirm whether or not he was telling the truth or trying to scare me into compliance. Doing what they wanted would only last until I could figure out a way to safely get Emma and Kaylee out of here with me.

There wasn't anything in the room that I could use to pry the wooden strips off the window, so getting out that way wasn't an option.

I knew how to operate a solarveyor, and the one Griffin used to bring me here had to be sitting outside. Even if I found a way to reach it, I wouldn't be able to get inside if he'd engaged the security on the access door.

"Who's Rygael?" Emma asked as soon as Conrad closed the door behind him.

I was relieved not to have the males scrutinizing me

anymore. The door might be closed, but the walls seemed thin, and I had a feeling Ian was loitering in the hallway. The last thing I wanted was for him or any of the other males overhearing my conversation with the girls.

I patted the bed beside me, encouraging the girls to join me. "He's my mate," I said, making sure to keep my voice low.

Emma moved to my left. Kaylee waited until she was sitting on my right before asking, "Is that like a boyfriend?"

"You could say that?" I wasn't sure if they were old enough to understand the significance of a mate, or the lifetime commitment made by a ketaurran male.

"Is he really going to come for you?" Emma asked, wiggling her feet.

"I think so." Though after hearing what Shane had planned for him, I almost hoped he didn't. The last time Rygael fought a male armed with a knife he'd been injured. I shuddered to think what would happen if he tried to take on four of them.

"If he does come to get you, will you take us to see Lily?" Emma pushed out her lower lip. "I miss her."

A door slammed somewhere inside the building, then a female voice echoed through the air loud enough for me to hear through the closed door. "Hey, which one of you guys stole another solarveyor and left it parked in the middle of the road?"

"Who's that?" I asked the girls.

"It's Tina," Emma said. "She's Shane's sister, but she doesn't come here very often."

Kaylee scooted a little closer to me. "She's way meaner than Shane."

"She was really nice at first. Told us she'd take care of us and everything." Emma picked at the fabric of her pants.

"Yeah, but after we got here, she locked us up, and told Lily she'd hurt us if she didn't steal stuff." Kaylee had way too much sarcasm in her voice for someone so young.

What was wrong with these people? I didn't understand how they could mistreat children or use them to commit criminal acts. I remembered the dagger I had stuffed inside my boot, the one Celeste had given me and wished more than anything that I could fight and wield a blade as well as she could. My friends faced situations worse than this one all the time and somehow managed to get out of them.

Footsteps, heavy and with a purpose, beat against the floor outside the room.

"Sounds like you were right about the lizard showing up after all," Shane said to Conrad as he shoved the door open and stepped inside again.

"What makes you think it's him? " Griffin hung back in the doorway with Ian returning to his place against the hallway wall.

"You don't think any male would be willing to give up a pretty thing like her, now do you?" Shane licked his lips.

He'd already demonstrated his willingness to exert control by making other people feel uncomfortable. I was surprised that he didn't grab his crotch as well.

"Even if you're right, how did he locate us? It's not like this place is easy to find."

"Lily knows how to get here, and after everything you told me, I was counting on her telling the lizard how to find the place." Shane proudly puffed out his chest as if he was a strategic mastermind.

"Move," Tina ordered when she appeared behind Griffin.

He hurried into the room to get out of her way. Her appearance didn't seem all that threatening. She was much thinner than her brother and a couple of inches shorter than his six-foot height. Her hair, a few shades darker than his, was gathered at the nape. But one look at her dark, menacing gaze, and I was certain Emma and Kaylee had been right about her temperament.

"If you're done gloating,"—she leaned against the door

frame with her arms folded across her chest—"then maybe you should get busy with the catching him part of your plan."

"Keep your pants on, Sis, I'm all over it," Shane growled.

"You better be," she huffed as she turned and left the room.

Shane walked over, grabbed my arm, and yanked me off the bed.

"No," Kaylee and Emma cried, trying to hold onto me.

"What are you doing? Let go." I struggled to pull free, but his grip was too strong. If Shane was right about Rygael's arrival, then I needed to help him, but I wasn't sure how.

"Don't get any ideas about trying to warn the lizard. Ian will be watching the little ones, and I'd sure hate for anything to happen to them because you didn't behave yourself." He took an intimidating step closer to the girls. "And you two better not give Ian any trouble, or I'll take it out on Harper."

Emma and Kaylee squealed, then reached for each other, forming a huddle of bodies and arms in the middle of the bed.

My dislike for Shane was growing more by the second. How many times had he used similar threats against the girls to get what he wanted? "It will be all right," I cooed, hoping to soothe their fear. "I'll be back soon, all right?"

"Okay," Kaylee lifted her head, trying to act brave for her sister.

I shot a warning glare at Ian as Shane shoved me through the doorway and past him into the hallway. My silent threat didn't seem to bother him in the least, but it sure made me feel a little better.

***

Rygael

Other than the building, there wasn't much Burke and I could use to conceal our arrival. A single viewing pane faced in our direction. Seeing inside or having anyone notice our approach wasn't possible because something had been used to cover it from the inside.

Once my boots touched the hard dirt at the base of the rocks, I raced for the back corner of the structure. From here, I could see the solarveyor I had heard slow to a stop next to the other two vehicles. I was surprised when a tall, thin female with dark hair stepped from inside and headed for the front of the building.

Burke had returned from checking the other side of the structure. "I don't remember Lily mentioning a female, do you?"

"No, but she was upset at the time, so maybe it was an oversight. Or maybe the female only comes here when Conrad takes Lily to the traders market."

"Either way, that's five people we need to deal with. And that's assuming Griffin and the other two males Lily mentioned are inside with Shane."

The odds were not favorable. Hurting a female went against my nature and everything I had been taught from the time I could walk. It was a choice I preferred not to make, but if it meant protecting Harper, I would not hesitate to do it. "It is not too late for you to change your mind about helping."

"What, and let you have all the fun. I've never walked away from a fight, and I'm not going to start now."

Since Burke had the training necessary for this kind of situation, I decided to rely on his expertise. "Assuming you are right, and everyone is inside, how do you suggest we proceed?"

Burke pulled out one of his blades. "If you can create a diversion, something that will draw one or two of them outside, I think I can get inside through the window on the other side of the building."

Living in the cave had taught me how to use whatever resources the environment provided to survive, so I quickly scanned the area for something I could use to start a fire. I spotted clumps of a foot-high purple plant I recognized growing near some boulders not far from the building. The tall, spindly blades provided forage for some of the sand-dwelling creatures. I also knew from experience that when the plants burned they created a lot of smoke.

"I have an idea." I pulled out my knife, then stayed low to the ground, hurried to the nearest clump, then swiped above the root.

"What are you planning to do with that?"

"Create your diversion," I said with a grin. "It is going to get really smoky very quickly, so as soon as this catches fire, you need to go."

I divided the plants in half, then cut two thin strips from the bottom of my shirt to tie around each bundle to keep them together. After snatching a small rock off the ground, I used it on the edge of my blade to create a spark. Once the end of one bundle started to smolder, I said, "Now." I ran toward the closest solarveyor and tossed the plant underneath it.

As expected, a cloud of purplish-gray smoke filled the air making it appear as if something had gone wrong with the engine.

I raced to the farthest vehicle and did the same thing with the remaining plant. Within minutes, shouting could be heard, then Conrad and Griffin rushed outside.

"Check the other vehicles," Conrad shouted at Griffin, then covered his mouth with his arm and knelt on the ground to look under the solarveyor.

There was too much smoke for him to see my approach, making it easy for me to sneak up behind him, then shove his head into the metal hull with enough force to render him unconscious.

Griffin stomped around the front of the vehicle. "There's no fire. It's a draecking..." He froze when he saw me.

I released a low, feral growl as I rushed toward him. I knocked him to the ground, straddling his mid-section, and gripping him by the throat with my free hand before he had a chance to pull his weapon. "Where is Harper?"

He clawed at my wrist and bucked with his body, trying to dislodge me. I was bigger and knew how to shift my weight to keep him in place. "Where?" I asked again, then pressed the tip of my knife against his throat.

His voice came out in a muffled squeak, his bulging eyes shooting toward the dwelling, letting me know Harper was inside. I continued to apply pressure, cutting off his air until he closed his eyes and stopped struggling. Although I would have taken great pleasure in ending his life, I was not the only one he had committed crimes against. I decided it would be best to let Burke determine the male's fate.

"Hey, lizard, if you're looking for your mate, she's over here." I pushed to my feet and glared at the male I assumed was Shane. He was standing on the platform near the front entrance, Harper's arm held firmly in his grasp.

I could tell by the expression on her face that his rough grip was causing her pain. Her clothes were disheveled, and some of her hair had pulled free from her braid. As soon as I noticed the bruise on her neck, I clenched the hilt of my blade tighter, trying to remain calm. Losing my temper would only make the situation worse.

"Harper, did they hurt you?" If I had seen anything but caring laced with anger in her green gaze, I would have been concerned that she had been harmed or violated in a way that was not noticeable.

"No," she answered, her hand instinctively going to her throat.

That alone guaranteed that I would not show the male

the same consideration I had shown Conrad and Griffin, that his life would end soon—slowly and painfully.

Since there was no sign of Burke or the female I had seen earlier. I feared his attempt to rescue the young ones had been unsuccessful, which meant I was alone in getting everyone to safety.

**

Harper

Shane had dragged me halfway across the building's sparsely furnished gathering room when Conrad blurted out something about a fire and raced outside with Griffin right behind him. All I could think about was getting back to Emma and Kaylee, so I could get them out of the building before it was too late.

Shane had ordered his sister and Ian to stay inside while he dragged me onto the platform to see what was happening. It hadn't occurred to me there wasn't actually a fire. Solarveyors were powered by sunlight, the engines not prone to lighting up in flames.

The thought of the threat being a distraction hadn't entered my mind until I was staring at the purplish-gray smoke billowing around the vehicles and glimpsed Rygael hovering over Griffin with his hand gripping his throat.

Once Shane made Rygael aware of our presence, he got to his feet, leaving Griffin's unmoving form on the ground. From this distance, it was hard to tell if Griffin was still breathing or dead.

"I need you to toss your blade aside and walk this way," Shane said.

The relief I'd felt at knowing he'd come for me was quickly replaced by the fear of what it might cost him, cost us. "Rygael, you can't." I tried to wrench free again. "He plans to sell you to slavers."

"He'll do exactly as I say if he wants to keep you alive."

Shane raised his knife inches from my throat, then called over his shoulder. "Tina, get out here, and bring those shackles with you."

A few seconds passed without a response, so Shane bellowed her name again. The front door slammed right before Tina came around the corner carrying a thick chain with wide cuffs attached to both ends. "Calm down, I'm right here." She dumped the chains in a heap next to her, then gave Rygael an up and down glance. "He's not much to look at, but I think you're right about the mercs paying a lot of cradassons for him."

Other than the tick in his jaw muscle, Rygael showed no sign of being affected by her remark. I, on the other hand, was furious. It was a good thing Tina was standing on the other side of her brother; otherwise, knife at my throat or not, I would have knocked her off the platform for insulting my mate.

"I'm waiting," Shane snarled at Rygael.

Rygael dropped his blade, only taking a few steps forward before stopping.

"Go chain him up," Shane ordered his sister.

Rygael growled, leveling a malicious glare in Tina's direction. For a female who didn't have a problem bullying others, I found it satisfying to see her back up a step. "I'm not going anywhere near him," she snarled. "If you want him cuffed, you can do it yourself."

Shane wasn't as easily intimidated as his sibling had been. Rygael raising a challenging brow, and purposely bating him, hadn't hurt either.

"Fine, keep an eye on her." Shane shoved me toward Tina, then grabbed the chains and marched toward Rygael. "Don't even think about trying anything."

"I would not think of it." Rygael taunted Shane with a grin.

"Put these on." Shane dropped the chains near Rygael's feet.

I wondered what Rygael was up to. It wasn't like him to

be so compliant, especially since Shane wasn't holding a knife to my throat anymore. Tina wasn't much of a threat, either. She grasped my arm but was too busy watching the males to bother pulling out her weapon.

Rygael kept his gaze focused on Shane, then leaned forward and grasped the pile of metal. Instead of attaching the cuffs as he'd been instructed, he swung the chain at Shane, the end wrapping around the wrist of the hand holding his knife.

Shane was too surprised to react when Rygael yanked him forward, then punched him hard in the gut, followed by an equally hard blow to the jaw. A blow that had Shane groaning and toppling to his knees.

"Hey, he can't do that," Tina said, releasing my arm and taking a step forward.

Did she honestly think Rygael was going to stand still and let Shane do whatever he wanted to him? I'd never seen Rygael fight but found his moves quite impressive. "Looks like he can."

She shot a sidelong glare in my direction and pulled out her knife. "We'll see about that."

Stepping out of her reach hadn't been necessary. Instead of grabbing for me as I'd expected, she jumped off the platform and headed for Rygael.

Tina's first mistake was assuming I'd be too afraid of Shane and her to do anything to stop her. The second was turning her back on me and going after my mate.

On more than one occasion, Rygael had demonstrated his natural instinct to protect all females. Would he adhere to his beliefs even if one was about to attack him? It wasn't a theory I wanted to test.

Running after Tina and tackling her while she was angrily waving a blade didn't seem like the smartest idea, so I leaned forward and slid the dagger out of my boot. All the throwing I'd done, which wasn't much, had been at a broader, stationary object, not a skinny moving one.

I'd never hurt anyone before and wasn't sure I wanted

to start now. I did, however, want to stop Tina before she got to Rygael. I held the dagger by the sharp end instead of the hilt and tried to remember every pointer I'd received over the last few days. After taking a steadying breath, I pulled back my arm and threw the blade.

***

Rygael

Disarming Shane had been satisfying and gone a lot quicker than I had expected. It had been easy to convince the arrogant male I would go along with his plan and get him away from Harper.

I assumed the female guarding Harper would pose a threat and had mentally prepared myself to deal with her. What I had not anticipated was hearing her screech as she jumped off the platform and ran toward me brandishing a knife.

Even more surprising was seeing my mate slip a dagger from her boot and throw it at the female. She clipped her in the back of the head with the hilt rather than the blade. The throw might not have been perfect, but the blow left the female lying face down in the sandy dirt several feet away from Shane.

"Rygael," Harper called as she rushed toward me.

I pulled her into my arms, thankful that she was alive and unharmed. "Harper..." I struggled to find the words to tell her how grateful I was that she had spared me from having to do something that went against my nature. Hurting a female, even one so evil, would have troubled me for a long time.

"I'm so glad you're all right." She rubbed her hands along my arms and chest. Once she seemed satisfied that I did not possess any injuries, she took my hand. "There are children inside, and we have to help them."

"Already taken care of." Burke strolled around the corner of the dwelling clutching a chain he'd used to shackle another male. He grinned even though his lip was split and bloodied. The male looked even worse. He had scrapes on his cheek, and one of his eyes was swelled shut.

"Burke?" Surprise flickered in her eyes.

"What took you so long?" I asked.

"I waited for you to draw the others out, so I could take care of this one,"—he shoved the forward—"and rescue the kids." He glanced back over his shoulder. "It's okay. You can come out."

Two small females who looked exactly alike peeked from behind him. "You're okay," they squealed as soon as they saw Harper.

She slipped from my embrace, then squatted to catch them in her open arms. "I told you everything would be all right, didn't I?" Once the hug was over, Harper returned to her feet. "Emma, Kaylee." She placed a hand on top of their heads after saying their names. "This is Rygael, my mate."

Kaylee tipped her head back and furrowed her brows. "You never told us he was so big."

Experience taught me that young ones were usually open and honest with their observations. I had expected comments about the lack of prominent colors on my scales, not my size.

"Who cares if Rygael's big or not? All that matters is that he saved us." Emma grinned up at me, then hurried forward to wrap her small arms tightly around my leg.

"Hey, what about me?" Burke's attempt to tease them with a pout was comical.

"Okay, you helped," Kaylee said.

"Do you want us to hug you too?" Emma asked, then giggled.

"Emma, Kaylee!" Lily shouted as she came running from around the back of the dwelling.

"So much for staying put," Burke muttered.

"I can't believe you two brought Lily with you." Harper's cheeks flushed, her glare leveled first at me, then Burke.

"She is not good with instructions." I gave Lily an admonishing look, then grinned. "But, we could not have found you without her."

"Well, in that case." Harper tweaked the end of Lily's nose. "Thanks."

Lily's gaze traveled to the female on the ground. "I wish I'd gotten here sooner. I would have loved to see you guys knock Tina out."

"Harper deserves the credit for rendering the female unconscious." I slipped my arm across the back of Harper's waist and pulled her against my chest.

She smiled. "I think my aim still needs some work, but at least I hit her."

"It was a beautiful throw." I pressed a kiss to her forehead. "One I truly appreciate."

She slipped her hands across my shoulders. "I'm pretty sure hitting someone in the back of the head with the wrong end of a blade doesn't qualify as beautiful."

"Eww, do you guys do that kissy stuff a lot?" Kaylee asked.

Burke chuckled. "Rygael, maybe now would be a good time to load up the prisoners, and get your family back to the settlement?" He didn't bother to wait for confirmation before leading Ian toward the solarveyor.

"I think that is a great plan. Kaylee, Emma, would you like to come home with us?" I wasn't about to leave the young ones behind, but I wanted them to feel as if they had a choice in where they would live next.

"Really?" Emma asked, glancing at Harper as if seeking reassurance.

"You're not just saying that, are you?" Kaylee skeptically studied me as she waited for an answer.

"Of course he's not," Lily reached out and took Emma and Kaylee by the hand. "Come on, I can't wait for you to see the house and meet the other kids." They hurried to trail after Burke.

Harper took my hand and pulled me to a stop. "Thank you for coming for me."

I cupped her cheek and smiled. "You are my ketiorra. I will always come for you." I brushed my lips over hers. The gentle kiss I had intended turned into something more passionate when Harper wrapped her arms around my neck.

My mate might not be a warrior, but she possessed the heart of one. She was a good dam to the children under her care, and though our home had grown by two more, I could not wait for us to have a young one of our own.

Thanks to Harper's compassionate and determined nature, I understood what it meant to have friends and family. I had a place where I belonged, but most importantly, I had a female I could cherish and share my future with.

ABOUT THE AUTHOR

Rayna Tyler is an author of paranormal and sci-fi romance. She loves writing about strong sexy heroes and the sassy heroines who turn their lives upside down. Whether it's in outer space or in a supernatural world here on Earth, there's always a story filled with adventure.